The 2010 Jersey Devil Press Anthology

Anthology

Edited by Eirik Gumeny

THE 2010 JERSEY DEVIL PRESS ANTHOLOGY

ISBN 978-0-9846127-0-3

All stories in this anthology have previously appeared in the online magazine Jersey Devil Press, with the exception of "Run Away" by Z.Z. Boone, "Nate and Adel" by Bruce J. Berger, "How to Tell Your Aunt and Uncle You Want to Marry Their Daughter" by Kevin Brown, "Mendelssohn Hinkle's One Thing" by Jonathan H. Roberts, "This is a Story About California and I Would Be Living There" by Jonathan Plombon, and "A Parking Space Fit for an Elephant" by Stephen Schwegler.

"How to Tell Your Aunt and Uncle You Want to Marry Their Daughter" originally published by Reed Magazine, 2009.

JERSEY DEVIL PRESS
Montclair, NJ

www.jerseydevilpress.com

In Jersey, anything's legal,
as long as you don't get caught.

— "Tweeter and the Monkey Man,"
The Traveling Wilburys

Table of Contents

The 2010
Jersey Devil Press
Anthology

The Legend of the Jersey Devil
Eirik Gumeny

For those of you unfamiliar with the legend of the Jersey
Devil, may I present to you the definitive myth, based
upon two hours of research and twenty-something years of
living in the Garden State.

But first, a little history lesson: In the 1700s there was no
electricity. There was no California, no Texas. Music
involved your family members singing at you from the
other side of your one room cottage. Magic was still a valid
excuse for teenage pregnancy, a farmer's inability to
harvest crops, lost luggage, and pretty much everything
else.

Which is why, in 1730, none other than Benjamin
"Motherfuckin'" Franklin published a story in the
Pennsylvania Gazette on the witchcraft trials occurring near
Mount Holly, N.J. And not in a "holy crap, you guys,
you're not gonna believe this" kind of way, either.

Okay. So. On to the story.

In 1735, Deborah Leeds, wife of Japhet Leeds and mother of
twelve, found herself knocked up yet again. Mrs. Leeds
briefly considered her options—which, at the time,
involved only birthing the baby and then either raising it or
selling it for meat—before throwing up her hands and
shouting, "The Devil take this child!" and then joining her
husband for a drink.

Lest you judge Deborah too harshly, you need to realize that the Leeds were not a rich family. Japhet was a local surveyor and a drunk, and Deborah was a woman. They lived, at best, a modest life in the Burlington area of southern New Jersey, on the outskirts of the Pine Barrens, and weren't exactly thrilled with the prospect of expanding their homestead.

The Pine Barrens, for those who aren't in the know, is a forest. A dark, desolate, scary forest, where the trees grow out of sand instead of dirt and actually need to be set on fire to reproduce. To this day it remains a largely rural, undeveloped area, in no small part because the crazy-ass ecosystem bankrupted a number of industries in the eighteenth and nineteenth centuries and then actually, physically *took back the areas that had been developed*. That shit ain't right, yo.

In any event, Deborah Leeds went into labor on an incredibly dark, violently stormy night. Tradition has it that Japhet and his twelve children were huddled in a corner of their tiny house, spooked by the crashing wind and rain and terrified of Deborah's promise to the Devil. More likely, though, they were sitting at the table in the next room, playing cards and trying to stay out of the midwife's way. The Leeds lived on a coastal town in the North Atlantic, near a forest straight out of *The Lord of the Rings*, with a woman who'd already fired a baby out a dozen times before. No part of this was new to them.

Well, not yet, anyway.

The midwife delivered the baby and, with strained enthusiasm, handed it to a yawning Deborah, saying, "Congratulations, it's a… a… oh my God! Oh my God!"

The baby, born a completely normal boy, suddenly changed. It began growing in size in the midwife's arms.

Horns inched out from its forehead and wings sprouted from its back. The midwife dropped the child and stumbled backward, watching as the infant continued its metamorphosis. It landed deftly on two cloven hooves; talons tore through its fingers and its face became that of a horse with glowing red eyes.

The midwife screamed in terror. Mrs. Leeds joined her. The creature roared.

Japhet got up from the table, ushering the kids beneath it. He grabbed the metal stoker from the fireplace and ran toward his wife in the other room, only to be smacked upside the head with the midwife's arm. Her torso soon followed. Japhet, a slow learner at best, made it all the way to the doorway before realizing that the beast had torn the woman to pieces. He stood terrified, staring at the unholy creature and trying to process what was happening. Then the monster lunged at Deborah. Japhet charged at the beast, brandishing his fire iron. The creature turned and bellowed at Mr. Leeds with an ear-piercing snarl, then threw him back into the other room and bounded after him. Seeing its brothers and sisters cowering in terror, it reared up before them, roaring and flapping its wings, before finally flying up the chimney and making its escape to the desolation of the Pine Barrens.

Again, as science hadn't been invented at this point, the above may be a bit of an exaggeration. There are some who argue that Mrs. Leeds' thirteenth child was, in fact, *not* a demon, but merely a disfigured, developmentally disabled baby, tossed out into the woods because people were assholes in 1735. Which may very well be true—and just as unsettling, in its own right—but it would make for one bullshit legend. And bullshit legends are simply not what New Jersey is about.

Since that fateful night, an untold number of stories about the Jersey Devil have been passed from generation to generation. Sightings of the beast have become almost as prolific as "What exit?" jokes and painful Italian stereotypes.

By far, though, the single most bitchin' tale of the Jersey Devil involves its becoming drinking buddies with the headless ghost of a pirate previously in the employ of Captain Kidd.

You see, in Barnegat Bay, in the late 1600s, Kidd buried a shipload of stolen cargo along the shore and then, as was custom, beheaded one of his crew members so that his spirit could stand eternal guard over the treasure. His corpse was left on the beach to, presumably, scare the crap out of potential looters.

After a couple dozen years, the ghost pirate got bored and went for a walk. Being a homeless spirit, he was, of course, drawn to the supernatural creepiness that is the Pine Barrens. He was just kind of hanging out there one day when this weird, horse-faced fellow came barreling toward him. The creature yelled and snarled; the ghost raised an eyebrow. The beast stopped in front of the ghost and they both stared at one another for a moment or two. Then they started laughing. They've been inseparable ever since.

There are plenty of other stories about the Jersey Devil, as well, involving naval heroes of the Revolutionary War firing a cannon at it, the former King of Spain running into it on a hunting trip, the fabled spree of 1909 that shut down schools and businesses between Atlantic City and Philadelphia, and a Long Beach fisherman who says he saw the Jersey Devil flirting up a mermaid.

In New Jersey, everyone knows someone who knows this guy who's totally seen the Leeds Devil. To this day, police in the vicinity of the Pine Barrens still receive the occasional phone call from drunken teenagers and lonely old ladies, claiming to have seen a winged creature with unearthly red eyes bounding through the forest. And to this day, police just laugh at them or politely assure them that they'll "get right on it."

Because they're all just stories.

Right?

Jersey Fresh
Kate Delany

You come home for a visit (your parents paid) and I pick
you up at the airport, of course. We hug tight at the
arrival's gate and I feel convinced and a little flattered.
Right away, you want to eat, famished and indignant about
the lack of anything fresh at the airport. You had pockets
stuffed with plums but they took them away when you
went through security. So we swing by the diner, which
couldn't be more like coming home, you say. It's the same
diner we killed so much time in as kids but now you revel
in the kitsch, telling me you're seeing with fresh eyes. You
just love how authentic and unpretentious everything is:
the hyper-laminated menus, the dumpy wait-staff, the
enormous windows with a view of the highway on one
side, of a brick wall on the other. A mother in a nearby
booth swats her whiny kid and you point, grinning, saying,
no one would ever do that in Cali. No way! Now I'm
definitely home! For several minutes, you marvel over the
chocolate chip muffin on the menu which no one, you
insist, would ever eat on the West Coast and that's what's
so great about being back here! No one gives a shit! I place
my order with our waitress, a girl you don't recognize but
who went to school with us, who works here nights and
weekends while her mom watches the kids. You interrupt
my "just a bagel and cream cheese" saying, "wait, aren't
you vegan yet? Why did I think you were? Still just
vegetarian? Huh." After you order scrapple, eggs, toast,

you say, really, I should do it. I should become vegan. It's
so much healthier, so much better for the environment.
When you get back to Cali, you're going to become a raw
foodist. Do I know about raw food, you ask? You tell me
it's the new thing. Nothing above 114 degrees. So pure, so
fresh! You tell me about a friend who made you a raw
dessert the other day and it was so simple, so delicious.
You can't wait to get home and get started, actually. You're
saying this as your breakfast arrives. You dig in, shoveling
in scrapple, blinding the eyes of the sunny side up eggs on
your plate. Of course you don't actually have any cash on
you so you put the whole thing—eight dollars—on a credit
card. As for the tip, with a dramatic little flourish, you
loosen your scarf made by some Tibetan monks and rope it
around our waitress's neck, muttering shanti, shanti. After
you head outside to bum a smoke off an old man leaning
on his walker, who just looks so Jersey, you tell me, I press
a fresh five into our waitress's palm. I watch her ball it up
in her hand. Anything that fresh, she tells me, you gotta
crumble up a little or else it sticks.

The Golden Streams of Babylon
Andrew Frankel

I was desperately in need of a piss so I ducked into The
Burrito Palace. There were many people inside; I asserted
my way to the counter and asked the girl behind it where
I'd find the bathroom. She shook her head, saying that it
had been out of order all day. I swore aloud.

"But there's a unicorn out back, in the alley, who's
just begging to be pissed on. You should go piss on him."
She smiled, sexy.

This struck me as terrible, but I knew that I'd heard
her right.

"But why?" I demanded. "Why would anybody
piss on a unicorn? In an alley?"

The girl narrowed her eyes at me and spoke in a
tone at once sharp and vague.

"You'll see," she said.

Out back, just a quick moment later, I was having the time
of my life pissing on the unicorn in the alley. I looked at
the heavens and laughed a hearty laugh. When I'd rushed
into the alley and come upon this unicorn, I'd realized at
once that the Burrito Palace girl had been right. Here was a
unicorn who truly was just begging to be pissed on; he
spoke with a pissy rasp and had that defiant "piss on me"
look set hard in his eyes. The soot all over his coat and his
Cockney accent suggested to me that perhaps he was a

down-on-his-luck chimney sweep, one who had fallen from grace for the sake of cheap thrills.

"Well, what's this then? Man about town, out for an evening piss?" He winked.

"You bet your unicorn ass," I said.

And I pissed on him. I think it delighted us both. After, we had a seat, he in the piss and I beside it, and smoked cigarettes.

The unicorn seemed to revel in a feeling of contentedness. He swayed, spoke of summers he'd spent in his youth. When he paused to sneeze, I asked his name.

"Larry," he said, "Larry Green the Third, sir."

"But you're red," I said, chuckling at the small irony.

He turned his Cockney unicorn eyes to the night sky and drew long at his cigarette.

"That's because I'm a bloody failure."

He sniffled, coughed, and spat on the alley floor.

I felt as though maybe I ought to say something to Larry Green the Third. His change in mood had been abrupt; perhaps he was unstable. It had occurred to me earlier that this probably wasn't the first time he'd been pissed on today.

"Listen, Larry. It's not all that bad. You know. Maybe you just need a change of scene."

Again he sniffled. His gaze looked thoughtful and I followed it, and saw two policemen rushing toward us with angry faces.

In the jailhouse, there were strange biblical screeds and illustrations scrawled on the cell walls. I considered them. Maybe I had gone wrong somewhere. I had never intended to get locked up for something like this. Larry smelled like pee. The charges were public urination and eliciting a lewd act in public, respectively. Larry looked crushed when they saddled him with his charge, and I understood. There was nothing sexual about what we had been up to in that alley when the policemen happened by. Just a unicorn who wanted to be pissed on, for reasons that were his own, and me obliging him.

"But why are you locking us up?" I asked the policeman. "Can't we just pay our fines and be on our way?"

"Yeah," Larry added defiantly. I glared at him, wishing he would shut up for a while. He'd started running his mouth as soon as they cuffed us, and I felt this could only affect our situation negatively. They don't much care for Limeys in these parts.

It turned out my feelings of anxiety were not unfounded, as the cop got up from his desk, pulled his gun from his belt, unlocked the cell door and proceeded to savagely pistol-whip Larry. The unicorn collapsed and spit blood on the cell floor; the cop turned to me but I only shook my head and raised my hands. He returned to his desk and reclined into his seat, a look of disdain and repugnance on his face.

"The reason I'm locking you boys up," he said, "is I don't like the idea of some freak and some unicorn roaming the streets of my city and pissing on each other in alleys. I don't know where you degenerates come from, but that's not how we do things around here."

I felt the need to defend my honor.

"Sir! Please, listen! This unicorn never pissed on me! The girl at the Burrito Palace said their bathroom was out."

And then I stopped. How could I make this policeman understand my story? Until I'd tried it a few hours ago, I myself had never dreamt of the thrill that came with pissing all over a willing unicorn.

Larry spoke up again.

"Listen, please. Do you have any Three Dog Night?"

The policeman turned slowly to face him, pulling his pistol and leveling it at the piss-soaked Cockney. Larry shrunk into the back of the cell. For a long time no one spoke, and I took advantage of the silence to try to clear the tequila from my mind. There was no way in hell I was spending the night in this damned cell. The smell was almost too much; it would have been too much already if the piss on the unicorn had belonged to anyone but myself. I've always prided myself on the clean, somewhat minty aroma of my own urine. But a fat lot of good that urine had done me tonight.

Some hours passed and, failing to come up with anything intelligent to say to the policeman to clear our names, I decided to get a little sleep. I was dreaming about a cat that turned into a spider and wanted to bite me when I awoke to a quiet beseeching from Larry Green the Third.

"Shut the fuck up," I hissed at him. "You've gotten us into enough trouble already. Just go to sleep. We'll figure something out in the morning."

"But look," he whispered, pointing a hoof toward the cop's desk. The policeman was dozing, his feet up on the desk, left hand tucked neatly into his pants.

"What's your point?" I demanded.

"We have a chance."

My gaze met his, and I fell headlong into his crystal green eyes. All of a sudden, my bladder was furious, ready for action. I guess one more couldn't hurt, I thought to myself, and instructed Larry in whispered tones to assume the position. Then, very quietly, I pissed on him once more.

With the morning light came the changing of the guard. The new officer reviewed our paperwork and stared at us a while. At length a smile cracked on his round face. I feared trouble. He sauntered over to the cell door and cleared his throat.

"Well," he drawled, "I imagine you boys have about learned your lesson by now." He looked me in the eyes, and there was a flicker of something like kinship behind his glasses. "You pay your fine, you can be on your way. A hundred dollars ought to do it."

I felt as though a great load had been lifted from me, and for a moment I was filled with happiness at this fortuitous turn of events. Then I heard Larry shuffling around beside me. It occurred to me that the policeman had said that I was free to pay my fine and go; there had been no mention of Larry's charges.

"Well, then," Larry began, trying to sound casual. "How much will this little adventure be setting me back?"

The policeman looked Larry up and down, the slightest trace of a smirk detectable on his face.

"Well, son, your charge isn't quite so light as your friend's here. But seeing as you seem to be an intelligent enough unicorn, and Cockney, I think we could work out some sort of work release program for you."

Larry hesitated.

"Work release?"

The policeman opened the cell door and beckoned to me to step out, telling Larry Green the Third to sit tight a moment. I paid the cop the hundred dollars and retrieved my possessions, and he told me good-heartedly that he hoped it would be a while before we met again. As I left the jailhouse, I turned to look at Larry one last time. He winked at me as the policeman entered the cell with him, hand to his fly.

After that night, I did a lot of soul-searching. It seemed to me that my life was headed in the wrong direction. Unicorns, Cockney accents, nights spent in jail—what was I hoping to accomplish, traveling such a path? I decided to go straight. It was really hard at first. The urge would rear its ugly and relentless head on certain nights, and I wouldn't know how to assuage it. Once I cornered a cat behind a warehouse and pissed on it, but it wasn't the same. And the hurt look in the cat's eyes as he ran away afterward had burned straight to my heart, telling me that this was not the way. No, I told myself, harshly. This will be the last time.

I went to see a therapist the afternoon after the episode with the cat. He listened to my story with his back turned to me, gazing out the window at a lush courtyard below. When I'd told all I had to tell, he waited a while and then spoke.

"You know," he began, "your story is not such a unique one. Since the dawn of man and unicorn, the temptation has been there. And many great men were known to urinate on a unicorn or two at some point in their lives. Abraham Lincoln, for example. And Donny Osmond."

I was relieved to hear this. He went on.

"The thing is, all of these men, sooner or later, came to realize what you must come to realize. Pissing on unicorns won't solve your problems. No matter how great the thrill, that is all it will ever be. Look out this window. There's so much life to be lived out there, and it'd be a crime to piss it all away. Even on unicorns."

The therapist's words struck a chord deep inside me. He was right; it was time to pull up my fly once and for all, and step into the sun. But first, there was someone I had to find. I thanked the man sincerely, left the office, and headed downtown to the Burrito Palace.

It was night by the time I reached my destination. Again it was busy, and again the same girl stood behind the counter. I could tell by her eyes that she recognized me.

"Well, hey," she said, eyelashes fluttering. "I was wondering if I'd see you again. Was I right about that unicorn or what?"

For a second I was overcome with nostalgia, but I fought it back and spoke.

"You were. But it was all wrong."

She gave me a look that said she didn't understand.

"What do you mean?"

"Listen," I said. "Have you seen that unicorn? I need to find him. It's hard to explain. Has he been in?"

"Yeah," she said with a confused smile. "About a week ago."

"What did he say?"

"Not much really. He ordered a bean burrito and three margaritas. Then he asked to use the bathroom."

My eyes widened at the mention of the bathroom, but again I beat back the wave of longing and asked the girl: "And then he left?"

"Then he left."

"And he hasn't been in since?"

"Not while I was here."

I felt at a loss, thanked the girl and on an impulse asked if I could use their bathroom before I was on my way. She handed me the key and I made my way back and unlocked the heavy door, flicked on the light. I couldn't believe what I saw. A giant mural drawn with a thick red pen spanned the entire wall behind the toilet. There was Larry Green the Third, rolling on his back in ecstasy. And there I was, pissing on him with a celestial smile. The drawing was crude, but in a way I'd never seen anything so beautiful in my entire life. The mural was signed, at the bottom, with a brief note.

"Drew," it read, "here's wishing you well, and a little something to remember me by. We lived like kings in our time, but every king's reign must sooner or later come to an end. I'm hanging up the old piss racket, and I hope you will too. Keep looking for grace, and I know someday you will surely find it. Until then, keep the faith, and stay dry. Larry."

I reread the note a few times, then shut off the light and left the bathroom. Never before had a unicorn so changed my life, nor has one since. When I handed the key back to the girl at the counter, she flashed me another sexy smile.

"You want to go ice-skating later?" I asked her.

"Sure," she said.

Run Away
Z.Z. Boone

It wasn't the way you heard. I know what the newspaper said, with its blaring headline declaring, **WILD GIRL FOUND**, but it wasn't like that at all.

What it was was this: my parents had divorced a year ago, my dad—a college professor—had followed a teaching position to Kansas State, and my mother had jumped back into dating like a penguin into the Arctic Ocean. We've had our share of problems over the years, Mom and me, but the atomic bomb really fell when she brought home Chuck Shea, had him move in with us, and announced they were getting married in October. I'd met the guy a few times before, and he was a shit. Then one night, while my mom was at her book club, the slimy creep actually tried to put his hands on me while I was making pizza in the microwave. As far as I know, he still has the burn on his arm where hot mozzarella met flesh.

I don't even remember what the big fight with my mom was about. I just know it was a Saturday afternoon, soon after July 4th, and my mother and I had had it with one another. She probably told me I should be happy for her and Chuck, and I probably said she was marrying a pig, and she probably said enough with the smart mouth, and I probably said I'd be better off someplace else, and she probably said well don't let me stop you. In any case, I was out the front door—sneakers, cargo shorts, and t-shirt— fully intending (at the time) never to walk through it again.

To appreciate my side of the story, you need to be familiar with the landscape. I live—had lived—with my parents in a small, box-shaped house in suburban Connecticut. There are neighbors on either side of us, but we all appreciate our privacy. We're separated from the Wippermanns by a high stockade fence, from the Morinos by a thick pine tree line. All of my seventeen years on earth have been spent in this one place. We were not among the super-rich; my father made an average salary while my mom worked ten hours a week at a plus-size women's clothing store called Ladies At Large.

Behind our house is a small backyard which borders on Paramount Park. It's a town park, minimally supervised in the summer and totally ignored in the winter. According to the brochure that you can pick up as you enter, it's 300 acres of trees, hills, and a manmade beach with a twenty-five acre pond. I never measured it, so I'll take their word. That said, no one knows Paramount Park like I do; I studied it on foot in the summer, from my sled in the winter. I rode my bike along the narrow foot paths and I skipped along the seldom used equestrian trails. I knew, too, to be particularly careful in the fall when hunters would illegally come into the park to hunt deer and turkey. Mostly they depended upon the silence of bows and arrows, but occasionally shots would ring out so close that the dishes in our china cabinet would rattle.

A year-and-a-half ago, I'd found a tree stand not far into the woods. It was nothing more than a sheet of plywood, maybe four feet by six feet, at least twenty feet off the ground, bolted into the triangular fork of a tall oak. There were probably rungs lashed to the trunk of the tree at one point, but they were gone when I showed up. The climb up wasn't easy, and when I finally got there the stand was littered with cardboard coffee cups, some empty pint bottles that had once held alcohol, doughnut bags and other trash. When I climbed higher, into the crown of the tree, the view—which included my house to the north and Paramount Pond to the south—was spectacular. I cleaned up the stand, eventually went back with a rope which I tied around a strong branch, and told no one about my find. I visited regularly and considered stocking the stand with some supplies, but never got around to it. The following fall the hunters apparently returned, used the tree stand, left it a mess which I again had to clean up, and stole my rope which I was forced to replace. By the time the snow began to melt, they had once more abandoned the forest for warmer, more comfortable places.

My first night as a runaway was easy. I found the tree stand, now hidden by summer foliage, and climbed up to it. I tied off the nylon rope and dropped it. The end dangled maybe six inches from the forest floor, a ladder I could lower and pull up as the situation dictated. The evening was mild and relatively mosquito-free, and near the base of the oak was a soft, dry spot where I could sit and lean my back against a fallen maple. When it began to grow dark, I heard first my mother, then Chuck Shea, come out of our house, venture onto the apron of the woods, and call. "Dawn Marie!" they'd shout. "Enough! Get in this house right now!" or "I'm not kidding, Dawn! I know you can hear me!"

But it was clear to me that they couldn't have learned their lesson in this short a time. Had I gone home that first night, my story would have been little more than adult cocktail party chatter. You're-never-going-to-believe-what-she-pulled-this-time stuff.

So I stayed where I was. I slept in my loft that night, not comfortably but peacefully.

On Sunday morning I was awakened by the sound of Chuck moving clumsily through the brush. I climbed down the tree, threw the rope back up, and hid in a ravine that allowed me to run either uphill or down, depending upon his approach. He called my name—the anger was still in his voice—and I could see from where I hid that several other men from the neighborhood had joined him. They were noisy and disorganized and the only time they even came close was around noon when Chuck and one of his buddies met for a smoke. I was flat on the ground, behind an old stone wall that was probably once a property line, close enough to touch either one of them with a long branch.

"She's not out here," Chuck said.

"Most likely on her way to meet her father," the buddy said.

"Well, the little bitch can stay gone for all I care," Chuck said as he crushed his cigarette on a section of the stone wall so close I stopped breathing.

The rest of the day became like a gigantic game of hide-and-seek, and by early Sunday evening, when it began to rain, they all gave up and went home. I might have returned home myself, except that Chuck's loving comment renewed my determination. Stay out here another day or two, I figured, and my mother's relief would be so great, her realization so sharp, that Chuck would be on his way out the door before my first hot shower was over.

As I mentioned, Paramount Park has a beach with trucked-in sand and a fairly good-sized pond that's stocked with bass, and it's one of the more popular places for families to hang out on summer days. That evening, though—with gathering clouds and rumbles off to north— it was empty. Still, I waited until eight, the park's official closing time, before venturing over. By that time the rain was coming down with a vengeance and a wind had picked up. The tiny gravel parking area was empty, the metal shed that the lifeguards used to store their equipment was closed tight with a large combination lock passing through the metal loop of an equally imposing hasp.

At this point it hit me that I hadn't eaten in over twenty-four hours, and a day on the run can burn energy. In my rain-soaked clothes I was able to rummage through the trash barrels and find two still-wrapped salami and cheese sandwiches, as fresh as you'd find in any deli case. The pond itself is probably clean enough to drink from, but I'd peed in it enough times to have my doubts. Fortunately, I was able to dig out two partially filled juice boxes, along with a half-can of Sprite.

And then a break. The public restrooms, a divided cinderblock building which practically no one ever used, were left open. I ate in the cleaner of the two—the women's—seated on the plastic toilet seat inside one of the stalls. It was smelly and dank, but I was protected from the increasing downpour. I shed my clothes and wrapped myself, mummy-like, in a roll of paper towels that was left on the inoperative electric hand-dryer. The room was windowless, but I avoided leaving the lights on for too long just in case anyone—teenagers, most likely—would choose to ignore park rules and wander by after hours.

I slept on and off throughout the night but never deeply enough to surrender to dreams.

The next morning—Monday—I was awoken by the sound of an engine idling. *Shit*, I thought to myself, *it's the lifeguards. How am I going to sneak out of here without being seen?* After a few seconds, though, I could hear a vehicle pulling away, its sound eventually fading completely. I peeked outside and noticed that the rain had stopped but the sun had not even come up yet. I ditched my shredding paper towel suit, put my still-damp clothes back on, and ventured out like a mouse from a pantry. The park opened at 10:00 a.m., and I was pretty certain it wasn't anywhere close to that late. I hoped that the car or truck I'd heard had left a delivery of food outside the snack bar, but I found nothing. What did catch my attention was the wooden regulation sign that greeted people as they approached the beach:

NO DOGS, NO GLASS BOTTLES, NO ALCOHOL OR FIREARMS, NO DIVING, NO LITTERING, SMALL CHILDREN MUST BE SUPERVISED BY AN ADULT, ENJOY YOUR DAY.

Stapled on the sign itself were two flyers. The blue neon one caught my attention first, most likely because it had my picture in the center. *Have You Seen Me?* it asked above the photograph. Below was a physical description, a rundown of what I'd been wearing, and my mother's phone number. I considered pulling it down, but was afraid that might help give me away.

The second flyer—no more than a hand-lettered sheet of copy paper—said *BEACH CLOSED DUE TO POLICE RECONNAISSANCE OPERATIONS.*

I have to admit. I felt a certain thrill about this. They'd probably have a helicopter which couldn't detect me if I was in one of the restrooms. They might have search dogs, but I figured I could swim out to the floating wooden dock and hide beneath it. They might even have police boats on the pond itself, in which case I could probably remain invisible behind the waterfall up by the water inlet.

In fact, the chase was disappointing. In the days that followed, some planes flew overhead, but they may have simply been routine traffic from Danbury airport. Police with dogs did search the area but, as I later learned, the dogs they used had been trained to sniff out narcotics, not human scent. I avoided them easily. The hunt was half-hearted and went on for only a couple of days since, as I also later learned, people were convinced I was somewhere between here and the midwest in search of my dad. No one ever pointed out the fact that although I liked my father well enough, our lives together had never been an episode from "Father Knows Best." If I had been lucky enough to track him down, he'd have wasted little time in calling my mother and sending me back.

During the time the park was closed, finding edible food was something of a problem, and I was reduced to eating soggy pretzels, overly-ripe fruit, half-eaten sandwiches, and—yes—drinking from the pond. By Thursday, however, the beach reopened and the trash situation improved. Thursday night I feasted: fried chicken, onion rings, and a piece of peach pie nice enough to serve at a Greek diner.

Something else started to happen around this time as well. I discovered that I enjoyed living outside, scavenging for food and living in a tree, more than I liked so-called "civilized" life. The sun warmed me, the night concealed me, the wind helped me move where I wanted to go. Things that had meant so much before—the gaggle of electronic devices that clogged my room—began to seem purposeless. I couldn't understand why, night after night, I used to sit in front of the TV and watch things I'd already seen. Going to school, going to church, going out with friends—it all seemed kind of preposterous.

You might think that boredom would have been my biggest enemy, by it wasn't. My day revolved around foraging, staying dry, avoiding sunburn and insect bites, and staying hidden. I'd see wild animals from time-to-time, and occasionally have to hide from a hiker or dog-walker. These things were exciting and active and I sometimes felt as though I, along with nature, was involved in one huge practical joke against the entire human population of the planet.

Beside food I was beginning to collect things that were being discarded: plastic bags to keep things dry when it rained, a forgotten cotton beach blanket, plastic bottles for water storage, sticks and rocks for use as tools. Occasionally I'd pick a day old newspaper from one of the trash barrels, and once—after I'd been gone about a week—I read about myself. **LOCAL GIRL STILL MISSING** read the page two headline of an article which went on to explain that my father had been contacted by the police but was not a suspect in my disappearance. "The longer the girl is missing," a detective was quoted as saying, "the less chance that we'll find her alive." The account went on to say that my mother's "planned betrothal to Charles Shea" had been "postponed until the daughter's disappearance is put to rest."

Let me be honest. There would be times when I would miss my mother terribly. During those times, if it was still light, I'd climb to the crown of my tree and stare, sometimes for what seemed like hours, at the house where I used to live. I liked it best in the mornings, after Chuck had left for his job as a reinsurance agent—whatever the hell that is—and my mother would go about her life as well as she could. I knew it was Monday when I saw her carry our garbage cans out to the end of the driveway, that it was Wednesday when she came in with groceries, that it was the weekend when neither car left the driveway.

And sometimes, always when she was alone, she would come into the backyard, walk to the edge of the woods, and stare in as if she was waiting for an invitation. A couple of times she said my name, not loudly, but just enough so it carried. At those times it was difficult, close to impossible, for me not to call back.

After about a month, I stopped wearing clothes when I didn't need them. My lightweight sneakers weren't made for this kind of life, so I only wore them as protection—climbing up and down my tree, for example—when necessary.

Things weren't perfect; I made mistakes. Once, probably sometime in August, I slipped up in a major way. I was squatting like an ape, using a broken branch to dig a hole in the summer-soft earth, and wondering how hard it would be to establish a series of underground tunnels. Suddenly, I heard voices. I looked up and saw a couple—a man and a woman—who had wandered off the marked trail. The man's eyes seemed to lock with mine, and they both fell silent. After a second or two, I heard the woman say, "Jerry, what is that?" They were a good fifty feet away, and I was able to scramble—nude and covered with mud—deeper into the woods. I hid in the low branches of a thick pine, and neither saw nor heard them again. It would be months until I learned that they had related the sighting to the police, that their story had been scoffed at by the local cops who were convinced the pair had come across no more than a large raccoon, and that even wilder accounts—including tales of "Wild Girl" sightings throughout the state of Connecticut—would be reported and sworn to.

A couple of weeks later another near disaster, but this one turned lucky. It had been a particularly hot late-summer day and the beach had been packed. As soon as the two lifeguards—a girl and a guy that evening—had packed up, gotten into a jeep together and left, I was on the beach. There was a trash barrel on the way out, close to the lifeguard shed, where people tended to throw away the best stuff on their way to the parking area. The pickings were good that night, and my mind was on my stomach.

Again, the mistake of not listening closely to the environment.

I picked up the sound of the jeep returning just before it came into sight. I had no path of escape. To run toward the shed was to run toward the jeep. To dash across the beach meant at least several seconds of exposure. So I squatted behind the trash barrel in the hope they might drive by, onto the beach maybe, allowing me an easy escape.

They didn't. The jeep stopped less than twenty feet from where I cowered, and in a second the girl—a redhead I thought I remembered from school—got out of the car. The boy must have said something, because she turned toward him and I heard her say, "Because my wallet is in it, that's why!" She fooled with the combination lock a few times, yanked on it, and finally yelled over, "Is it *two* left or *twelve* left?!"

The boy stuck his head out the jeep window and called back. "Two left, twelve right, thirty-eight left!"

Bang. She was inside, out a minute later with her tote bag, back inside the jeep, gone.

And I had myself the combination to the lifeguard shed.

I let myself in a bit later that night. There was stuff I could certainly use—a first aid kit, a wooden box filled with hand tools, a small refrigerator with some cans of soda and someone's forgotten lunch—but the risk of calling attention to myself was too great. The important thing was that fall was coming. That in a month or two I'd need shelter, food, and heavier clothing. *I just screwed up big time,* I thought to myself, *but I think I may have found my shelter.*

But my biggest mistake—the one that would play a huge role in my downfall—involved my own stupidity.

Labor Day weekend led to the official closing of the beach. By Tuesday the picnic tables and trash barrels would be removed, the restrooms would be shuttered with plywood, the floating wooden dock would be pulled up onto the shore's edge.

It started off as a clear Friday morning. Warm, sunny, light breeze. From the top of my tree I saw my mother and Chuck, carrying overnight bags, come out the front door. They were arguing in a way I hadn't remembered seeing. "Put it to rest!" he'd tell her, and she'd shoot back with something like, "You have no idea what it's like!" Minutes later they were in her car and gone.

That day the beach was packed with people trying to squeeze in as much summer as they could. So I waited until well-after dark—midnight maybe—before venturing out. I dressed, carefully approached the house, found the front door key which was always kept hidden behind the coach light on the right side of the front door.

The entranceway light had been left on—my mom's measure of security. Still, I moved cautiously. I was immediately aware of foreign odors: chemicals, cleaning products, smoke and grease, maleness. I moved from room to room like a drunken woman in a house I could have negotiated blindfolded a couple of months before.

My mother is a scrupulous housekeeper; her routines are unbreakable. Anything out of place does not go unnoticed, so I fought down the temptation to grab and flee. I knew that she kept an emergency cache of canned goods in the basement—she added one or two each time she went shopping—and I felt sure I could filch a few without raising suspicion.

My bedroom was exactly as I left it. I carefully went through my dresser and removed a pair of flannel-lined jeans, a wool sweater, two pairs of heavy socks. From the back of my closet, I found a pair of suede hiking boots that I never wore. My winter coat is a full-length brown leather number, and there was a good possibility it might be noticed missing. But I needed to chance if I was going to make it through the winter, so I took it down and put it with the other clothes.

I never once considered taking a bath or trying to rake a brush through my matted hair. Those things leave traces. What I did do, though, was dumber still. I lay down on my bed, intending to rest just a short time, the softness more seductive than I'd remembered, and fell into a deep dreamless sleep.

I jolted awake the next morning, like an animal suddenly aware that it's wandered into a trap. The digital alarm clock next to my bed read 10:12. For all I knew, my mother and Chuck were on their way back—right now pulling into the driveway, perhaps. I straightened my bed, went into the kitchen, grabbed two paper shopping bags from the endless supply in the cleaning closet. In the basement, I took only cans with ring-pull tops: two sweet corn, two potatoes, one each beets, green beans, limas, Spam, and SpaghettiOs. I returned to my room and quickly packed up the sweater, pants, and shoes in the second shopping bag. The leather coat was too big to pack, so I wore it.

I turned out all but the entrance light, closed the front door, replaced the key. I felt like a thief which, in fact, I was.

Reentering the woods was like surfacing after too much time spent under water. Life, as the cliché goes, was good. I had shelter, warm clothes, food for a few days. I'd fashion a fishing pole and a spear. I'd not only make it through the challenging New England winter, I'd thrive.

The heavy leather coat slowed me down a bit, so that when I felt the pain in the back of my leg I figured it was little more than a cramp. But the feeling intensified, so much so that I first dropped one shopping bag, then the other before falling to the ground.

"Dad, I got him!" I heard a young male voice call.

When I reached behind me I felt the shaft of the arrow sticking through the back of my thigh. I was motionless. All I could do was lean my forehead on the damp forest floor, wish for the pain to pass, close my eyes and hope this was a dream I was having back in my own soft bed.

The hunters didn't stick around, but they didn't leave me to die, either. There was a call to 911 and I was—I'm told—carried out by stretcher and taken to a waiting ambulance on the beach. According to one newspaper report, the people already on the beach formed a semi-circle around me as I was lifted into the back of the ambulance. They were not so much concerned with my safety as they were with seeing this feral girl, her bloody leg elevated and girdled with bandages, finally captured and carted away.

Had I been shot by a grown man, or had the head on the arrow been sharper, it would have done more damage. In fact, it probably would have passed completely through my leg. Still, bone was struck, muscle was torn, nerves were severed. Now, two months and two surgeries later, I can walk with crutches, but doctors say my chances of ever walking upright again are slim. After my first surgery, some local people collected money and bought me an adjustable modular frame wheelchair with swing-away armrests. Others have volunteered to help construct a ramp next to our front porch steps and Fairfield Home and Lumber Center will donate all the materials.

My father visited while I was in the hospital, and promises to fly out again over Christmas vacation. I'm not a kid, so I don't for a moment entertain any thoughts of him and my mom getting back together.

Speaking of my mom, the fight I heard between her and Chuck that morning was—as they say—the beginning of the end. She returned from their intended Labor Day vacation alone, refused to talk about the circumstances, and never allowed Chuck to show his ugly face around here again.

A few teachers from school have come by the house and kept me up with my classes. They think I'll be able to graduate in June with the rest of the seniors, be able to go to college if that's what I decide.

It's getting on to November now, and the tree that I lived in all that time has multi-colored leaves to match its neighbors. The tree stand, I'm told, has been dismantled and taken down, and I'd like to think it was done as a preventative measure. Were it still there, other local teens might treat it like a shrine, or worse, be tempted to follow my example.

Sometimes, on milder days, my mom will take me outside in my wheelchair. She'll take me around back if I ask her, and turn the chair so I can stare out into Paramount Park. I study the terrain and note how far I'd get in my wheelchair—not even beyond the first tree line.

And even though my mom, always standing alertly behind me, probably knows as well as I that escape is impossible, I can sense her hands closing around the handle grips and holding on tightly.

This is a Story About California and I Would Be Living There
Jonathan Plombon

Chapter One

There is a college student who recites poems about trees. He can be seen every Tuesday night at that coffee shop where protesters go to celebrate that they stood outside for three hours and carried signs. He walks around with a cigarette in his left hand and a diary in his right. I read his diary when he was in the toilet. I read it because he was in there for a long time, and I honestly didn't think he'd ever make it out. But all I found in his diary was a grocery list that featured SpaghettiOs and orange juice. That was his most revealing work. It explained EVERYTHING about the previous fifteen minutes.

Anyway, he'd say to me, "Do you have any conceivable notion of how sadistically difficult it is to live in California AND maintain a semblance of integrity while birthing creative, intelligent, and thought-provoking work?"

Then he'd get inspired because he just noticed that tables are sometimes made of pine, and he'd say to himself, "Fascinating."

"I've been trying to get my collection of tree poems entitled 'Nature Is My Mother, Tree Is My Stay-At-Home Father, Pinecone Diapers—Hurt' published for three years now. And even I have yet to reach the heights of my idols: Jack Kerouac and Ernest Hemingway. Me. What (cough,

cough) [he wouldn't actually say *cough*, it'd be more like *arghhhh, arghhhhh* because people don't really say *cough* —author's note] moving, highly personal (har, har) [he'd actually say *har, har* and would probably do it with his fly down —author's note] literature have you bestowed upon our society?"

Then he'd walk away, presumably to write a tree poem because he would still be inspired by the whole tables-being-made-out-of-wood epiphany.

Then I would leave, too. Or buy a hot dog. It all depends on how long the line would be.

Chapter Two

I'd be able to make it. I know I would. Even without a series of autobiographical tree poems. Then when I win my first Academy Award, I'd raise that solidified naked man in the air and say, "Have you ever heard of a book called, 'Nature Is My Mother, Tree Is My Stay-At-Home Father, Pinecone Diapers—Hurt'?"

And when no one would say anything, I'd remark, "Yeah, I thought so. Oh, and yes, thank you, I'll accept all the other awards, too, even Best Actress. That's a tentacle to how great of a writer I am."

My Academy Award ceremony would be nothing like other things. For example, it would be unlike a person staring blankly at nothing in particular when he works at the pizza stand in the mall. And then when a customer asks for something and the employee doesn't get something, the customer remarks, "What are you waiting for? Do you want an award?"

And even though you really want that award that he speaks of, and you admit that "Yes, I do," it might get you really fired.

Chapter Three

Today, I will be handing in the first two chapters of my story to the creative-writing teacher at the community college. My teacher once informed us that writing is the most difficult skill to master. I raised my hand.

He said, "Yes, Jonathan?"

I said, "If that's true, why is it that everyone on the Internet is a poet but no one on the Internet is a brain surgeon?"

He said, "Just because someone says they're something doesn't mean they are."

He was probably right. It's probably easier to get away with writing a crappy poem and still be considered a poet than it is to get away with performing crappy brain surgery and still be considered a brain surgeon.

My teacher said that the class is "supposed to have three whole chapters ready." It made me wonder if a brain-surgeon teacher tells his class that they're "supposed to have three whole brain surgeries ready." But maybe writing is as hard as brain surgery, because I couldn't even get my writing assignment done. I only wrote two chapters. I'm stumped. Heaven knows what it would be like if I had to perform brain surgery.

My teacher once told me to "draw inspiration from my life." So I said, "Can I have a pencil?"

My teacher said, "You already have a pencil in your hand."

And I answered, "So I can *draw* inspiration."

This is my third chapter. I guess.

Chapter Four

"First of all," my teacher said. "The third chapter has nothing to do with the first two chapters. Second of all, your, um, structure is, um, experimental."

Then the class provided some feedback. I had nine people tell me that I had "great descriptions" and two people said that they "like SpaghettiOs too."

When I got the comment sheets back, a few people asked, "Where the hell is California? Isn't the story about what it would be like in California?"

I'm going to have to add more California. I see that SpaghettiOs are pretty popular, might have to add some more great descriptions of them.

Chapter Four

California wouldn't be all awards-getting. With success brings stress (that's what people who have never experienced non-success say). For instance, there'd be times when I'd get invited to parties and not be able to attend because other people wanted to schmooze me.

"You are invited to too many parties. Waaaaaaaaaay more parties than I'm invited to," Paris Hilton would tell me. "But you absolutely have to come to my birthday party."

"OK," I'd say.

"That's hot."

"Yep."

"(Click) (Beep)." [We would be talking on a cell phone —author's note.] [Not the same cell phone, but different ones. —author's other note.]

Now I'd have to pick up a tuxedo.

"You should pick one up at this hot new shop on Sunset Boulevard," rap mogul P. Piggy and his wife Miss Piggy would inform me over a dinner of creamy, circular noodles better known as SpaghettiOs.

Out I'd go, strutting to the Hot Tuxedo Shop on Sunset Boulevard. I'd see my friend Jennifer Love Hewitt. She'd smile. I'd smile. I'd call her *Love*. She'd probably call me, *Thomas* because it is my middle name [remember, *Love* is Jennifer Love Hewitt's middle name —author's note]. Or maybe she'd use *Plom* or *Bon* for some reason that (Jennifer) Love (Hewitt) would only know. But if she'd use those I'd be like, "Who the hell is she talking to?" I wouldn't know that she was talking to me. It'd be pointless. I'd tell her just to use *Jonathan*. It'd be our "thing."

After saying bye to Love (Jennifer Hewitt), I would be confronted with another peril of being a celebrity: the book-buying public that loves me. Someone, say, like the guy in the mascot outfit from Chuck E. Cheese or the "crazy" weatherman from K-CUD channel 12 can't be bothered when a fan sees them standing in line at Mostly Bun Burgers on Thirteenth Street at 3:34 PM on March 22, 2004.

These people have places to be. They are busy. They have meetings. They would, but they just can't. They are sorry. They thank you people for supporting them. They love each and every one of you. They couldn't do it without you. They ordered this hamburger without lettuce. They could buy and sell this place. They think that this place should be happy that they'd even go in this stink-hole. They want no ketchup and only some mustard. They want to know what your definition of *some* is. They don't care how many birthday parties you've had. They don't care what your name is. They just don't care anymore, screw it, hicks.

"I'm sorry—I'm late for a meeting with my agent. Pay for this," they say while sticking up their middle fingers.

"I'm sorry—I'm late for a meeting with my agent. Pay for this," I would say while sticking my thumb up to some guy who bought my book.

"I'm sorry—who should I make this out to?" I'd say to the girl with no bra and huge rack. "You like my book, eh? Well, I like yours, too. Mmmmm-hmmm. Like 'em like SpaghettiOs. I read it between the lines, baby. If you know what I mean, Spaghettiette."

That'd be really clever. Unless she answered, "Oh? You've read my book of tree poems?" or "How'd you know my name was Spaghettiette?" Then it wouldn't sound so clever. It'd just be a good guess.

Chapter Four

I handed in the new chapters in class today. My teacher was surprised that I kept in those two chapters that had nothing to do with anything. Now in order to preserve continuity I have to write other chapters that have nothing to do with anything so the entire story makes sense.

This means that I'm changing the plot. It used to be about a guy who is super popular and lives in California. But now it's going to be about a guy who is super popular and lives in California and is writing a story about it for his creative-writing class at the community college at another time in another state who may not be the same person.

My teacher looked over the story and shook his head.

"Well, how about we try this. I want you to go home and find the last great piece of literature you've read. It doesn't need to be a novel, just something like a short story or newspaper article that you enjoy, and I want you to try to write like that author. Look at how it's structured and imitate it."

The only reason I remember all of what he said is because, after he finished telling me it, he said, "I don't know, I just don't know, let's try this" and wrote it all out on a sheet of paper.

I think the last thing I read was the back of a cereal box.

Chapter Monkey

I'd go to pick up my date. I'd know which one was my date because she wouldn't ignore me when I said hi to her in the hallway. In fact, she'd be a hi-saying girl. I've met many of them, so I'd be able to identify one almost immediately.

Also, my date wouldn't come up to me, dance with me, then turn to her friends and laugh. Never.

And I'm not at liberty to disclose the identity of my future date. She doesn't know that she's my date yet and if she found out that she was herself it would lead to big problems.

In the meanwhile, I've already written many poems about my future girlfriend. Here's an excerpt from one of them:

> I've eaten hamburgers
> and I've eaten fries,
> Tasted shakes
> and swallowed pies,
> Your body's shape never fails
> Why don't you respond to any of my e-mails?

I feel very close to this poem. But not so close that I wouldn't still sell the movie rights to it. In *Variety* there will be a full-page article saying, "Jonathan's done it again with hit stanza; Michael Jackson not surprised."

Chapter Five

I'd want to make out with my girlfriend on the way to Paris' place, but the limo driver would still insist on talking to me.

"You know, it is quite remarkable how famous and successful you have become, Mr. Plombon. Especially when you consider that you've done it without writing a single tree poem. My wife loves you. And my wife is one of those women who has never had acne and never had to worry about acne disfiguring her back and making her feel really awful."

I have heard how much acne can scar and make people uncomfortable with themselves so I would know exactly what this guy's wife would not be going through.

"Your back, by the way, is really clear of blemishes; it's very attractive," the limo driver would tell me.

"Tell me something I don't know," I'd whisper.

"You are so bad," my date would say.

"Chill out, baby. I know my complexion is perfect. I don't need anyone telling me. I'm a brain surgeon and a writer."

Chapter Six

Corn flour, sugar, oat flour, brown sugar, coconut oil, salt, sodium citrate, nonfat dry milk, whey, partially hydrogenated soybean oil.

Chapter Seven

My teacher didn't even read the rest of my story this time. He just told the class, "I want the last three chapters of your stories by the end of the next class time, and I want twelve in total by the end of the semester."

I tried to tell him after class that he forgot me, but he ran out of the room without his briefcase and coat. When Julie said something about it, he screamed, "I forgot my car keys, too; I don't know how I'm getting home."

Chapter Eight

William brought up that the chapters in my story aren't numbered correctly. And to make matters worse, I numbered one chapter *monkey*. I don't know what a chapter monkey is, but I know it can't be good. On a more-positive, less-scary note, these chapters are becoming easier to write. This one took three minutes.

Chapter Eight

I'd arrive at the party and all the people would greet me. There would be Lindsay Lohan, Nicole Richie, Hilary Duff, Christina Aguilera, Dick Tracy, Madonna, Chester Cheetah, Jennifer Lopez, and He-Man (Spudz McKenzie would arrive late).

This party would be nothing like when you send a MySpace message to a girl that you know from class. You really need to know when an assignment is due, but then she doesn't write you back. The next day you visit her MySpace page and she's made it private. It would be nothing like that.

Chapter Nine

The waiter would ask me, "Mr. Plombon, would you like some champagne?"

"Of course," I'd say, turning around. "Haha, write a fucking poem."

[Oh, the waiter would be the tree-poem guy. I forgot to mention that. —author's note]

Chapter Twelve

After the party would die down, I'd walk to the balcony and stare at the Hollywood sign. With its constant flow of light extending beyond the building and struggling to maintain its current ascent in the afternoon, the sun would cast an alphabet shadow on the grass. My date would grab me from behind.

"I love you," she'd say.

I'd cry, cry like when a person is recognized by one of the pretty, popular girls that he went to high school with and even remembers my name.

Chapter Monkey: Return

One thing I learned in creative-writing class is that you shouldn't add characters or plots and then never acknowledge them again. Thus, the chapter monkey returns.

Chapter Monkey: Dead

One thing I learned in creative-writing class is that there should be a resolution for each character. That's why the chapter monkey died [it was suicide, and he used chimpanzee poison by mistake, but it still worked —author's note].

Anyway, it was the final day of class. I got a star on my story and a "Good Job!" Great, except that everyone else got actual letter grades and not just vague compliments. Plus, I had forgotten to hand in my finished story so my teacher just gave me back an article from yesterday's newspaper about a boy who won a spelling bee.

My teacher told the class that if we feel strongly about our stories that we should submit them to a publication. I'm submitting this one to *Jersey Devil Press*. I read that one of its main criteria for accepted submissions is quality. Check.

I've got it all. Resolution? Check. Continuity? Check. Drawing from personal experience? Check. Great descriptions? Check plus.

Nate and Adel
Bruce J. Berger

Smoke curled up lazily from the ashtray where Adel had placed her cigarette, adding to the haze that always seemed to permeate the small two-bedroom walkup where Nate tried with difficulty to make a home for himself and his daughter. The noise from 53rd Street seemed unusually quiet for a Saturday afternoon, but Nate assumed that many of their neighbors in Borough Park were doing as were he and Adel, watching or listening to the Dodgers game. In the Miller apartment, even with a small television set in the corner of their tiny living room, the preferred method was to hear the ballgame on the old radio that Nate had owned since before his only child was born. They both loved the voices of Vin Scully and Red Barber and loved to imagine their heroes on the field rather than watch them through the grainy, ghostlike images of the television.

The game had not been going well for the Dodgers. Billy Loes, the Dodgers starting pitcher, had pitched out of a jam in the first, gotten through the second giving up only a walk, but in the third two quick singles in front of a mammoth home run by Wally Post put the visiting Reds ahead by three runs. The Dodgers escaped further injury only when Carl Furillo rifled a strike from right field to Don Hoak at third, nailing Gus Bell, who foolishly had tried to pick up an extra base with two outs.

Adel had chain smoked through her pack of Marlboros, but she did not seem anxious in the least.

Instead, she focused on the announcers' voices emanating from the radio and kept meticulous score in the notebook that she used to track all of the Dodgers games. Between innings, during the Schaefer Beer jingles, Adel closed her eyes and hummed off-key.

After the top of the fourth, Adel turned to look at Nate and giggled.

"Adel, what are you hearing?"

"He says that I'm beautiful and that he wants to marry me."

"Who's saying that today, sweetheart?"

"Jackie Robinson, of course. And he says that the Dodgers will win it in the ninth inning. He didn't say how, though."

Nate sighed. It had been three years since the advent of Adel's illness and two years since Louise had left. For the first 16 years of her life, Adel had been, not only normal, but brilliant, a straight A student. Nate thought that she would follow his footsteps into law. And then, overnight as it seemed to Nate, Adel lost interest in school, started eating voraciously and gaining weight at a monumental clip, took up smoking, heard voices that no one else could hear, and often garbled her speech. Occasionally, she would dig her fingernails into her body until bloody streaks appeared. Adel would moan and claim that she was being eaten by insects crawling under her skin. To prevent serious injury, Nate and Louise tried to keep bandages wrapped around the ends of her fingers.

Of course, Nate and Louise had tried to get medical help for Adel, but the doctors turned out to be useless. Five doctors agreed that Adel had schizophrenia, but with that basic diagnosis came no acceptable treatment advice. One doctor claimed Adel's hormonal balance was off and that she needed estrogen injections, but another doctor said just the opposite. When Nate and Louise couldn't get any straight, consistent answers, they decided not to fool with drugs. One doctor recommended electroconvulsive therapy, an idea that sickened them, and two others told them that Adel's disease had no cure and that they should just put Adel into a psychiatric hospital for the rest of her life, an idea that sickened them even more. Adel's parents sadly that somehow they would have to take care of Adel without professional help. But as the three of them wound their way to the end of the string of consultations, Adel's condition worsened and Louise began to lose interest.

In her only episode of violence, Adel had gone after Louise with a knife, screaming that Louise was the devil. Even given Adel's oddities, the attack struck Nate as out of character, and Nate could never really figure out what had led Adel to go after her mother. Never particularly stable herself, Louise had always been hypercritical of Adel, and, as Adel's serious mental problems mounted, Louise had been less and less able to cope. On the day in question, Louise managed to escape harm by locking herself in the bathroom until Nate got home from work and discovered the pathetic tableau, Louise crying in the bathroom, Adel sitting on the sofa muttering and periodically punching herself in the head, the bread knife lying beside her.

Nate managed to coax Louise out from her hiding place and tried unsuccessfully to piece together the story. His wife began packing her suitcase, still sobbing, protesting that she had "had enough" and would say only that she would be moving back in with her mother. The next morning she called a cab, not bothering to say goodbye to Adel and merely yelling over her shoulder at Nate that she'd be in touch.

The contacts between them since had been sporadic, and Nate couldn't be sure when he'd last spoken to her. Adel hadn't seemed to mind that Louise had left, hadn't even seemed to realize why she had left, quite content to interact only with Nate, never mentioning her mother. After the initial shock of her departure, Nate adjusted well, he thought. In a way, he felt relieved that she was gone; he could now focus just on Adel.

Nate continued his work as a wills and estates attorney in downtown Brooklyn, hopping the streetcar five days a week, and otherwise devoted himself entirely to his daughter. He gave up his weekly Tuesday night pinochle game to be able to stay around the apartment more. He stopped going to the neighborhood synagogue on Saturday mornings, instead using that time to update his stamp collection, using the kitchen table as a workplace after Adel had cleared the breakfast dishes. Every spare minute of his time he used to monitor Adel in the apartment or take her out with him on carefully controlled activities: a trip to the zoo in Central Park, a long walk downtown with a streetcar ride back, and an afternoon or an evening in the bleachers at Ebbets Field where they took in as many Dodgers games as Nate could afford. For the most part, Adel conducted herself so as not to attract attention, but every now and then she might strike up a nonsensical conversation with a surprised bystander until Nate apologized and pulled Adel away.

At the start of the 1955 baseball season, the voice that Adel heard intermittently became that of Jackie Robinson. Nate had no idea why her mind had fixated on Jackie, although, as the first Negro major leaguer, he was certainly famous enough. Nate knew that Jackie was well past his prime, however. He wondered if Adel knew that as well. When Nate had attempted to point this out one morning over breakfast, Adel withdrew into her strange mental world and had no intelligible response. Jackie would "talk to her" at all times of the day or night, and he could often hear Adel "talking back." He might hear a one-sided conversation such as "That's right, Jackie. [pause]

I'm with you. [pause] I'll see you at 3 pm. Bring Rachel. [pause] Why aren't you playing more? [pause] Better have a doctor look at that heel." If he asked Adel what she was talking about to Jackie, more often than not Nate would receive a puzzled glance from Adel and no further information. Nate couldn't even bring himself to ask Adel why Jackie Robinson's wife often figured in her hallucinations.

And then, breaking into his drifting train of thought, he heard Red Barber's excited Southern twang:

> And there's a line drive into the gap in right center. It's going to the wall. Snider heading around third and they're sending him home! Furillo digging for third! Here's the throw! Safe! Triple by Furillo, Snider scores, and the Dodgers are finally on the board!

Adel made a few notes on her scorecard, and Nate was pleased to see Adel smile, something that she rarely did, even though the Dodgers had been winning most of their games lately. The smile grew in the bottom of the sixth, when the Duke hit a homerun and another run scored on two singles sandwiched around an error, bringing the Dodgers even in a 3-3 tie. Labine took the mound for Loes. The teams traded runs, and the score remained tied at 4 as the Dodgers came to bat in the bottom of the ninth, when Adel advised Nate that either the Duke or Furillo would hit one out. Afraid to ask how she knew, Nate just listened.

Vin Scully had the call:

> The small crowd here at Ebbets Field on a beautiful Saturday is on its feet. They're trying to make noise, but there's only about 6,000 fans. Duke steps into the box. He's one for two with a sacrifice today. Homered

in the sixth. Ooh, there's fastball on the
inside corner. Strike one. Duke doesn't like
the call, turns back to glance at umpire Arty
Gore for a second. Cincy reliever Hersh
Freeman now winding and pumping and ...
ball outside and upstairs. He'd better bring
that down or he's going to get punished. 1
and 1 the count. Duke steps out, knocks dirt
out of his cleats, takes a big practice swing. ...
OK, he's ready. Here's the 1-1 offering.
Swung on, long fly to right ... foul. Count
goes to 1 and 2. Duke got good distance on
that, but the wind helped push it over to the
wrong side of the foul pole. Now Freeman
ready to deliver again and ... swung on! Deep
to left center, Bell running back to the track,
he looks up, and that ball is gone!

The sound of the cheering crowd, small or not, could be
heard clearly over the radio as Scully stopped announcing
and just let the noise of Ebbets Field carry over the radio
waves.

"Hot damn! Jackie told me they'd do it in the ninth
and they did!"

Adel was now beaming, jumping up out of her
chair, skipping and twisting her great bulk around the
room, pudgy arms lifted, her hands raised over her head in
happiness. Nate could not help himself, but got up as well,
caught Adel, and gave her a mammoth hug. He was
shocked both because Adel had divined how the game
would end and because her happy reaction was as strong
as he'd ever seen. Her euphoria lasted only a few minutes,
however. Before the out-of-town scores could be
announced, Adel had retired to her bedroom, and Nate

could hear her slamming her pillows around and talking to someone unseen.

***

Two years passed in much the same manner, Adel always hearing the voice of Jackie Robinson, even after Jackie retired at the end of the '56 season. Nate and Adel gloried in the Dodgers' World Series win against the hated Yankees in '55, suffered when they lost to the Yankees in '56, and suffered all the more in '57, when the aging Dodgers failed to play up to their potential, falling out of first place for good in early June. Somehow, Jackie seemed to talk to Adel in the games that the Dodgers would win. She directed her speech intermittently to the great Negro baseball player in her head and to her father sitting nearby.

"He says Drysdale is going the distance today. I like him, too, Jackie. Dad, the bullpen will get a rest."

When Adel, listening to the game on the radio, had nothing to say about Jackie, Nate came to expect that the Dodgers would lose, and they often did.

During the summer of '57, more than just the Dodgers' lackluster play affected their fans in Brooklyn. Rumors that had begun the year before of the Dodgers leaving town for Los Angeles continued to fly. Whenever Adel heard or read references to the growing likelihood of Brooklyn losing the Dodgers, she reacted by kicking at imaginary beasts around her chair and pawing the living room air around her head with her hands, as if trying to catch something fleeting and ephemeral. The Dodgers began playing some of their home games in Jersey City. Out of curiosity, Nate took Adel across on the ferry on a warm Wednesday afternoon in August to see the game at Roosevelt Stadium, but her perpetual scowl and incomprehensible mutterings, as well as embarrassing him, told Nate that she had not enjoyed the experience. The Dodgers lost to the Giants and fell further behind in the pennant race.

Nate knew that the Dodgers were leaving and nothing could prevent it from happening. Yet, desperate to do something to cheer up Adel, Nate decided to take Adel to a meeting of the "Keep the Dodgers in Brooklyn Committee." After making their way downtown on a Thursday night in September, they discovered to their horror that, including the two of them, there were only five people in attendance. The Committee had no plan, no resources, no leadership, and no meaningful public support. Adel cried all the way home, a response that Nate felt was more than rational.

In early October, after the season ended, the inevitable occurred. The News headline told it all: "Bums Jilt Brooklyn for L.A." Adel screamed when she saw the headline, took off her shoes, and started beating them on the windows of the apartment. Nate wrestled them away from her, but she started punching herself in the head. With difficulty, Nate grabbed her in a big bear hug, restraining her from further self-inflicted injury, and kept her locked in that fashion until her violent straining ceased and the only movement of her body was the shuddering of her sobs. When it seemed safe, Nate lit a cigarette and placed it gingerly in Adel's mouth. As she began to suck in the hot smoke, her crying faded, but she still would not speak. For maybe the hundredth time in the past five years, Nate called in sick, afraid to leave her alone.

***

For days on end, Adel refused to leave her room for any reason. Nate had to find a chamber pot so that she could relieve herself, a pot that he cleaned twice each day with heavy disgust. He would bring her meals on a tray, but she would only nibble on a piece of toast. Although she had a lot of extra pounds to lose, her rapid weight loss could not have been healthy. At times, she would mumble her end of a conversation, and Nate would occasionally hear the name "Jackie," but could not understand more than that. He wracked his brain for some strategy that would pull Adel from the terrible depression into which she had fallen.

In early November, Nate read in the News that the Dodgers were shipping out all of their baseball equipment from Ebbets Field on the following day. He sat at the kitchen table, reading and drinking his daily cup of tea, trying to envision what was involved in stripping down a baseball clubhouse and moving its salvageable contents across the country. Lost in thought, he picked up a pen and began doodling on the sports page, drawing first the sketch of a baseball field, then the sketch of a truck, and then a circle around the truck meant to be a wall or a moat, some impassable barrier. The pitiful sound of Adel's crying penetrated his consciousness, and he went to her room

The room was dark, only a sliver of the morning's light making its way past the shades covering the north-facing window. Adel lay on her bed, her wool blankets pulled over her head, so that the only part of her visible to Nate was one foot extending out from the large lump.

"Adel, it's Dad. Do you want to talk?"

"What's to talk about?"

It was almost the first thing that Adel had said in a week. She sniffled once, and then the crying seemed to stop. Nate was encouraged.

"I know what's bothering you. Have you... been talking to Jackie about it?"

"I haven't heard him in a long time, Dad."

"Adel, you need to get out of here. I think you need to go to Ebbets Field and accept the reality of what's happening. Do you think you can go with me tomorrow morning, early?"

"Why? What's tomorrow?"

Nate told Adel about what he had just read. He somehow felt that witnessing the tangible departure of the Dodgers' equipment from Ebbets Field was the only thing that could motivate Adel to leave her dismal room. And he knew that his strategy, such as it was, bore substantial risks. He feared that Adel could fall into an even deeper depression from which there would be no recovery. He feared that Adel's mental derangement might worsen; perhaps she would become violent again, perhaps she would lose all contact with reality. As it turned out, the idea appealed to Adel. A few minutes after Nate left her room, she emerged herself, emptied her own pot, and used the bathroom. Another encouraging sign.

Early the next morning, Nate woke Adel, helped her bundle herself into her winter coat, and led her to the streetcar that passed Ebbets Field. It was Adel's first venture out of the apartment in a month. She was quiet and expectant. When they disembarked at Flatbush Avenue, Nate and Adel walked around the now dormant baseball park until they saw a large truck being loaded at one gate. They also saw that a small crowd of reporters and news photographers in overcoats and fedoras had gathered around to watch the event. Two uniformed policemen stood chatting and laughing together on the fringe of the crowd. Nate led Adel up through the pack, and they stood watching for a second. He could overhear one of the reporters he recognized as Dick Young complaining to the photographer next to him.

"What a dumb waste of time. There's no story here. What am I supposed to do? Talk to the truck driver?"

The photographer nodded, not even bothering to point his camera at anything.

Nate whispered to Adel, and then the two of them walked up purposefully to the front of the truck. Adel lay down first, directly against the right front tire, and Nate followed quickly by lying down next to the left front tire. They lay head to head. Immediately, the reporters and photographers scrambled around, being handed the story for which they had so desperately hoped. The two police officers moved closer as well, waiting to see what would happen.

"Hey, what are you guys doing?"

Flash bulbs popped, their noise punctuating the chilly air. Nate, looking up, could see a dozen faces of men in black and grey looking at down at him. All seemed to be asking questions at once. Twisting his head, Nate saw that Adel's eyes were clear, even sparkling. She began to speak, and the crowd quieted momentarily.

"We have been sent here by Jackie Robinson. Jackie says that the Dodgers are not allowed to leave Brooklyn. He says that we are going to lie in front of these trucks forever to prevent the Dodgers from leaving. This is my Dad here. He's a lawyer."

Flash bulbs continued to pop, and the questions from the reporters mounted together into an indecipherable crescendo.

"You know Jackie?"

"He talks to me all the time."

"Hey, is that really your daughter? She's nuts, right? You're nuts, too, right? What's your names?"

Nate dutifully gave the reporters their names and then, after another few seconds, stood up slowly. He helped Adel to her feet. He held her hands and looked her squarely in the eyes, moist with tears not yet fallen, but still clear and accepting. He spoke to his daughter from the depths of his heart, hoping to reach a tiny part of her that was still rational. He spoke in a louder than necessary voice, slowly, so that the gaggle of reporters would be able to get down every word.

"Adel, I don't think we can stop this from happening, as much as we'd like to. But your speech was beautiful. And I'm betting that our pictures will be in the News and the Post. It's time to go home."

More flash bulbs popped. Nate did not know how much Adel comprehended, but she remained calm, squeezed his hands, and smiled. They started back towards the streetcar stop, ignoring the reporters following them with more questions.

At the corner, Adel lit a cigarette and resumed one of her imaginary conversations.

"OK, Jackie, we've done it. The Dodgers are staying in Brooklyn. [pause] Say hello to Rachel and give my best to the kids. [pause] Sure, I'll marry you. [pause] I love you too."

The reporters, guffawing and elbowing each other, finally finished scribbling in their notebooks. They left to return to the truck, still waiting to carry its precious load away from defunct Ebbets Field.

Nate and Adel looked up Flatbush Avenue to see if a streetcar was on its way, but saw none. Suddenly, Adel pulled him towards Alsamet's Deli.

"Come on, Dad, I'm starving. While we're waiting, buy me some kosher hot dogs."

He bought four, happily giving her three and keeping one for himself.

You and Me and the End of the World
M.R. Lang

"So… what do you want to be when you grow up?"

***

The recent graduates from Eastly High School started to gather at the park hours ago. It was decided that tonight shall be the party to end all parties. Because, not only is today the last of high school, it is the last day. By the time the party's over, there will be no more parties. Whether or not they all know, nobody really cares. The two to survive the night, we shall call, Adam and Eve.

***

Eve stops dancing on the edge of the sidewalk for a moment to think.

"Remembered… loved… the last one standing."

She takes another moment to consider what she'd said. She closes her eyes and raises her arms in victory.

Adam keeps staring at the page taped inside the store's window: "HELP US WELCOME REBECCA BACK TO OUR FAMILY 6/24." His eyes stay on the note as he turns his face towards Eve.

"Hey. Rebecca's back."

"Who's Rebecca?"

"Don't know. But I feel reassured knowing she's back."

A car blows by Eve going at least 50 and the two almost meet in a very awkward way. She shuts her eyes lightly and savors the wind. Adam leans into a light pole and watches with a smile.

Adam looks as the bank's digital thermometer turns into its digital clock.

"We're going to be late. Let's go. We'll miss the good freaks."

Stopping her twirls, Eve walks backwards to the car outside the pharmacy, and leans the back of her head on the roof.

"I'm not going."

He turns to leave, knowing she'll be right behind him soon.

"It's the end of the world. Of course you're going."

***

Sara transferred to the school a few months ago. Her "use your rules to go fuck yourself" attitude won over classmates who thought she was "nu-punk" which meant something to whoever said it first. In reality, Sara's just a punk. She goes to the parties because there's always booze and usually drugs. She gets them free. When she doesn't thank you for them that means you're cool.

Eve pulls on Adam's sleeve, as if that's the on switch for his ears.

"Why are we walking towards Sara? She hates everyone."

"I like people who hate everyone. Very relatable. Good liars, too."

Eve goes to the opposite side of the picnic table Sara's sitting on and grabs one of the drinks Sara didn't thank anyone for.

Sara mostly ignores Eve, but turns a cocked eye towards Adam.

"What are you guys doing here?"

"Avoiding responsibility."

Adam nods to a wristband on Sara's left arm. If nothing else, accessories tend to bring attention. Sara wasn't one for attention, really. Then again, someone like Sara knows how to cut one's wrists properly. A horizontal cut along one wrist must be Sara's way of saying, "oh yeah?!" Whatever the answer is to that questions is, it isn't "yeah!"

"I was trying to… shave… my watch…"

Eve stands and turns. Grabbing Adam's jacket, she walks them off.

"Well, better luck next time."

***

When they woke up yesterday, they both knew. The world would end and whatever comes after would begin. Selected by God, Fate, sheer force of will… they don't take the time to consider it. Why the world ends, how it will end, why they'll survive… doesn't seem to matter. Even if the flow happens to be in the molten steel coming from the skyscrapers that used to live in Main City up north, go with it. Adam can't stop his nose from whistling when he breathes too hard. Eve can't even stop the ends of her hair from curling up when it gets too long. The end of the world is over their heads. The world will end, and they will watch.

***

Alan and James had taken down the Christmas lights from one of the gazeboes in the park, and are now replacing them with 9-volt batteries and many small strings of wire.

Eve tiptoes up on the outside of the gazebo and gets her finger up close to a battery to see how hot it is.

"Where'd all the batteries come from?"

James kicks the box full of 9-volts.

"Smoke detectors. Snagged on our way here."

Adam chuckles.

"I guess the chance that the fire finally starts the night two toasters steal the detector batteries are slim."

"Eh," Alan scoffs. "It's my stance that if a fire starts, the race needs to remember 'fire bad' without the piercing beep noises. Otherwise, Baby Darwin cries."

Eve touches a battery and jumps back a little.

"So, uh… why?'

"Is pretty," Alan moans.

"Never thought you two would be much for aesthetics."

Adam offers Eve his cup of what tastes like paint thinner and sadness to cool off her finger. She dunks her finger in the cup and takes a swig.

"We're seeing if it can get hot enough to actually start a fire."

James puts a battery to his tongue to see if it's alive enough to use.

"It's an expression of anger, irony, and boredom. Mostly boredom."

"I'd say it's mostly irony."

Adam watches Eve's face as she tries to figure out what she just drank.

"Irony and 9-Volts. Should totally be a cover band."

"Electronica covers of Sixties folk songs. We are Irony and 9-Volts," she sneers with a rock sign, the now empty cup hanging from her singed finger.

***

They didn't bother with graduation or the last day of school. Anyone else who survives won't care if you have a diploma. They'll just be happy if you'll share your water or aren't a zombie foraging for brain meats. They spent the last two days of recorded history together. Watching their favorite movies and shows in case it's the last chance. Talking about the advantages of living in a post-apocalyptic world. Such as the destruction of Wal-Marts, Starbucks, and L.A. No more ring-tones, no more spam, all the Twinkies that will never grow old. Survivor: Earth. There were jokes about that Twilight Zone episode where that guy's glasses broke.

The scariest thing about the end of the world is whether or not you and your loved ones will survive. Adam and Eve have nothing to be afraid of.

***

Amy is both the only student this year to have a parent in World War II and to graduate at sixteen. Seeing her father now makes her think of all the kids to be born to old, decrepit couples living and having sex far, far beyond their years thanks to modern medicine. Amy thinks modern medicine should cure young, poor people before making rich, old people live despite their decaying innards. She also drinks heavily.

Jay pierced his left eyebrow at the start of freshman year. People say he did it to make people think he was punkrock.

Later that year, he started walking around school with a cigarette behind his ear around teachers. People say he did it so people would think he didn't care. Sophomore year, Jay got a tattoo of a lion pouncing on his right wrist. People say he did it so people would say he's tough. For a time, he wore a beaded dog collar. For another time, he'd speak with a fake, Madonna-English accent. People never say that Jay likes to control what people think about him, but if they did, they'd finally be right.

Alison was a cancer survivor by the age of eleven. It was touted as a miracle and the doctors all told her she was very lucky. Every time she's screwed up since then, her parents yell and scream about how she's living her second chance, and about how most people aren't so lucky. After cooling down, her parents always try to make up for yelling with a gift, and her friends all tell her how lucky she is. Alison spends a lot of her time on Internet journals and forums trying to console terminal patients. She watches specials on TV about good people who are dying from illness. For the last seven years, Alison has never once felt lucky. Every breath makes her feel guilty for surviving.

Ryan thinks about friends who died when he wasn't around. Steven cries himself to sleep thinking about the horrible people he knows who will all succeed him. Jamie signed her name with hearts until her boyfriend betrayed her with a word.

***

Standing across the street from the park, Adam and Eve watch their former classmates and co-inhabitors of planet

Earth. They dance, they drink, they be merry despite themselves.

"God," she sighs. "They all look so happy. I hope we won't have to bury them."

"I wouldn't worry about it. We're about to inherit all the Febreze in the world."

Adam produces a small flask from his jacket, and fills Eve's little cup back up.

Eve coughs out a little laugh, trying not to cry.

"Toast?"

"Here's to the end of the world."

They drink and squeeze in close.

The car that almost hit Eve earlier flies by them and the park, seemingly going nowhere. The car's stereo pumps out the bass that's probably from a song, but no one can tell for sure. The car's left headlight goes out as it hits a mailbox up on a curb. The car's driver suddenly crashes from his amphetamine high. The driver's car suddenly crashes from the driver's amphetamine crash. Neither survive the night. Somewhere, a gazebo burns. Really, it signifies nothing.

Adam looks at Eve. Eve looks at Adam. The fires start. The world comes to an end.

Navels
Ansley Moon

Maureen was in the business of navels. She didn't pierce them, she didn't paint tattoos on them, and she wasn't a delivery nurse that cut the umbilical cord. No, she just loved navels.

Something about them reminded her of the embryonic stage of life. She was sure she could remember her life in utero and the Hendrix, Dylan, and Joplin played during her last trimester.

Every day she would see one navel. It wasn't as if she was looking for them, they just seemed to appear, after all she did live in New York City. Whether it was some baby squirming out of its clothes, some teenage girl in a risqué midriff riding the subway and nursing a cigarette behind her ear, some construction work using the front end of his shirt to wipe his brow, some promiscuous woman barely wearing anything or some guy in Duane Reade reaching for something and exposing his bare belly. Granted, some days there were more than others, like on Friday or Saturday nights or on sweltering city days.

She had even begun compiling a book about navels with photographs. In it, she explained the physical difference between the "inny," "outy," or "combo," as she called it. The first photo she took was a photo of her own belly button, a small brown outy that she contrasted with a white tank top against her dark skin. The rest of the photos came in spurts. There would be days when she would forget her camera and see the most beautiful navels. And there would be other days or even weeks when no one would allow her to photograph.

Maureen decided to sign up for a nude drawing class. She had no propensity for nudity or drawing, but she figured she could coax at least the model into letting her take a photograph.

When she got to the address, she pulled her slip of paper out of her purse and checked the number on the building. There were no signs posted. It must be to keep the freaks and the perverts away she thought. She opened the glass door and walked up the five flights of stairs, her heart pumped hard in her chest when she reached the last flight of stairs. She sat in the back and pretended to draw until class was over. After class, she walked up as the model was tying his robe. She blushed and he agreed.

The final take was stunning; his belly button was a cute, flat inny, outlined by a small trail of dark hair.

She took the class two more times, resulting in one photo of a popped pregnant lady's honey-colored navel, and one woman who refused to have her photo taken.

In the winter she finished her book. It included photos of innys, outys, and some combos, big navels and small ones, some scarred ones, black ones, caramel-colored ones, dark brown ones like hers, white ones, pink ones, yellowish ones, fat ones, flat ones, jeweled ones, tattooed ones, pregnant ones, hairy ones, even some scary ones.

She put all the originals into an old shoebox, and crossed out the word Tattoos and wrote N A V E L S underneath in black ink. Then, she placed the box into her closet on top of two other shoeboxes, one that read T-Shirts, and the other, KNEES.

Big Girl
yt sumner

I'm getting bigger.

Andrew wags his tail and it thumps on the floor. Andrew's big too, he's an Irish wolfhound and that's the biggest dog in the world. I know I'm bigger because my yellow dress is tight and it was baggy when I first got it. That was when Mum was watching the TV a lot and always frowning. She'd say shoo, when I tried to look over her shoulder and see the fires and the bad men.

Mum said not to worry and not to watch the TV. But just before she went to get help, the TV and the lights went out for good. It's not that bad though. The red sky hurts my eyes a bit in the day, but it's real pretty at night. Like a nightlight's always on.

Mum's been gone to get help for a long time. I don't know how long but I find an advent calendar to count the days. It's one that shows Christmas in the snow, like it was in England. I stop counting the days after I eat baby Jesus.

I sleep a lot.

I'm T-Rex. I'm a lizard king. I start in an egg. I grow a tail. My teeth get huge. I scratch out and I hatch. The sky isn't red and howling. It crackles like the sea. A bath big enough for me to swim in. I get hungry so I start to eat. I get bigger. I munch on little dinosaurs that munch on leaves. My tiny claws pick their bones out of my teeth.

I wake up a bit upset because I don't even eat meat and hide my tears in my pillowcase. But then I remember Mum isn't here anymore so I get up and brush my teeth. I keep scrubbing until the taste of baby dino is gone then I go out to the porch to check on the speck.

Mum said to watch for the speck. Watch carefully and make sure it's help before I run out and wave them in. She told me about the bad men and how they were hungry and I said I could just give them some cans and she reached up and held my chin and said if the bad men came, they wouldn't want cans. I had to run the other way. Into the black trees and ugly bushes.

At first I was excited about all the cans in the basement. I stacked them up against the wall in the kitchen as high as I could. There's lots of spaghetti. Most days I walk around the house eating spaghetti worms out of the can then I watch the horizon. I watch for the speck of dust that is going to grow like a thundercloud between the black peach tree and the well. Mum said not to go near that either. That I might fall in.

One night it rains. I love the sound it makes on the cracked tin roof. But I love it more on my skin. Boom. Thud. Smash. I run outside and Andrew is barking next to me. The sky is the darkest red and I run under it. I dance around on the black dirt and I yell that I'm a big girl. The biggest in the world. Andrew is barking and he starts to howl and growl he runs near the well and I run after him and put my hand out to grab his wet fur but he snaps at me. I say don't be scared Andrew but he runs for the gate. He runs and he doesn't look back. Something in the rain sounds like it's screaming and I run inside and hide under my bed the best I can fit.

Andrew doesn't come back.

Things were sort of okay with Andrew still here, even without Mum. I didn't like being told by other kids that Andrew wasn't a good name for a dog. I don't remember anything else about school and I wipe my eyes and eat some spaghetti. I don't know why I stopped going to school. Maybe I got too big.

I wait for Mum to come back. Or Andrew. I don't like spaghetti as much as I used to. But I still eat it, and it's nice to paint the empty cans when it rains. I don't like the rain as much either.

One night I dream there are angels at the window. They spread their wings and tell me a story.

> *You were born on a night where the moon*
> *was full and pink, just like fairy floss, in a*
> *room where silver sparkles tickled the clouds,*
> *trapeze angels flew and danced in celebration,*
> *and when you came out you didn't cry, you*
> *just smiled, and you said hello. You were the*
> *biggest star of the show.*

I wake up and smile. If the Circus came and found me they would be so proud of how big I'd got. Then we could go and find Mum. It starts to rain and I cry a bit because somewhere out there Andrew is scared too. I get up and paint some cans with the colour of his fur. I paint one with his big black nose.

In the morning I find a lizard on the porch.

He's baking in the sun, a little sizzly steam coming off his back and I pick him up to say hello and he breaks. Right in two. I hold his squiggly tail as he slithers off. I feel a bit sad. That he would rather break than sit in my big hand. Also that my dress tears in a couple of places when I bend down to pick him up. But mostly because he breaks. I take the tail inside and I put it inside one of my Andrew cans. He already had four legs and big floppy can ears. When I stick the tail on the end it wiggles and wags and he looks pretty happy.

Now I'm glad the lizard broke.

The Andrew cans start sleeping in my room, he comes for walks on the porch while I watch for the speck. But last night I forgot to bring him in with me.

The Circus is coming. They sing songs and do cartwheels. The Alligator Man snaps his teeth. The Fat Lady sings. They throw spaghetti worms into the air, and I look down and see that they're really lots of tiny lizards, and they all have Andrew's head.

I wake up and my hair was sweaty and it's the morning. My legs don't hurt. But they're so long. I get up and hit my head as I walk out of my bedroom. I think maybe the house shrunk a bit when I was asleep. I grab a new can and go out to the porch and sit on the steps next to Andrew. He's watching the horizon and something's different. My eyes feel funny. I open my can and see they're pears.

I look at the pear tree.
And see it.
The speck.
Finally.
I step off the porch and my toes get dusty. I run to the gate, right by the well and the speck gets bigger. Maybe it's Mum, I think. But it starts to make a sound.
The Circus is coming!

I yell at Andrew Cans and he wags his tail so hard it flies off.

I clap my hands and wave them in but then a sound comes from the well.

Help.

I lean over the edge and look into the black.

Hello?

Help.

Mum? What are you doing down there?

I put my ear right over the hole but Mum doesn't say anything else.

It's okay, Mum, the speck is nearly here. The Circus is coming to help us.

I walk back to the gate and wave my arms up high. But as it gets closer, Andrew Cans comes closer and whines a bit, he clatters as he shakes.

It's okay.

I say as I smooth my tight yellow dress, bursting at the seams.

I'm going to be the star of the show.

Run for the Border
Louis Wittig

Jim Manzlyk did not see the cop car idling under the lamp post in the parking lot on his left. Or his Grand Am's speedometer, or the blinking yellow traffic light, or the curb. He saw the Taco Bell and when it filled the windshield he slammed the brakes.

Hurtling out of the car he grabbed the restaurant's locked front door with both hands and jerked back with all his weight. He sprinted around back, praying under his breath and sweating everywhere else. The drive-thru window was dark. Still, he wheezed up to it and peered in. A perfunctory fluorescent bulb hidden deep in the kitchen dropped threads of pale light along the edges of wire shelves and sleeping registers. Jim pushed up onto his tiptoes and wrestled back his breath so he wouldn't fog the glass.

He needed an angle or shape or clue or anything to surface from the shadows and show him that this was the Taco Bell he had been at two days ago. He would have settled for anything that suggested it wasn't one of the six other Taco Bells he'd tried since midnight. He just couldn't tell.

It was at that same time of night, years ago, that Jim had pulled in to a rest stop on I-90 for a Coke. As he waited in line to pay, an old man sidled up next to him and claimed that his brother-in-law swore that he could taste the difference between bottles of Coke.

"Like they were bottles of wine. Can you believe that?"

No, Jim couldn't. But the old man's eyes had grown in anticipation of Jim's answer, so he said the man's brother-in-law should work for Coke, as a taster.

"Oh, he died years ago," said the coot, unmoved. "Heart attack."

This memory floated up underneath the silhouettes of upturned chairs and stacked trays like the ghost images in those Magic Eye puzzles that eluded and humiliated him for a brief period in the '90s. Higher on his tiptoes now, Jim's calves were burning. The thought slipped out that all these places were identical.

He knew that wasn't true. It had been the day before yesterday, driving down Central Avenue after lunch, when Jim had seen the cheddar orange blur of a Taco Bell roof out of the corner of his eye. It was unexpected and obscured behind a Mr. Subb he knew well. It must have been new. Jim had already eaten, but it had been forever since he'd been to Taco Bell. He turned around at the next light.

Before he got up to the counter he was already thinking he should leave. Just from the walls—lush red and irregular like hand-smeared clay—he suspected that he'd wandered into an unadvertised line of members-only Taco Bells. The windows flared into Mission-style arches with crosses at the top. Between the windows, framed black and white photos of single clouds in desert skies and soulful pottery forced him to consider the alternate possibility that Taco Bell had been bought out by a chain of art galleries. Either way, he was about to head back to the door when he saw the only other customers: Two black kids, boys, one older and one younger, leaning over a table, concentrating on a wordless game of rock–scissors–paper.

"Welcome, sir," said a voice from behind, jangling Jim. "Is there any way in which I might help you?" The voice had a British accent.

Jim turned around and the man behind the counter put down the lint roller he had been working over his uniform. He looked like Santa Claus' aristocratic older brother—slimmer, with a cleaner, closer beard—but every bit as sincere; maybe more. His nametag said Gordon.

"We're serving our complete menu today," Gordon chuckled.

Jim ordered a chicken quesadilla combo with a crunchy taco: a pure reflex.

"Excellent, sir. You are number 175," Gordon nodded towards the pick-up end of the formica bar. "Shaniqua will serve you shortly." Gordon resumed his grooming.

Jim meandered down-counter, running his fingers idly along the condiment station and bringing them up cleaner than they'd gone down. He noticed the two boys weren't playing anymore. The older one had curled up into a peanut on the seat and fallen asleep. The younger one had disappeared.

"175."

Shaniqua called it out like a nickname she had made up for him. Jim looked up and beheld her. She was so lithe and perfectly proportioned that if she had been playing an employee on a Taco Bell commercial, he would have taken it as insult to his intelligence. She held his tray out to him with elegance. And just as he took it, the small boy darted out from where he'd been huddling behind her leg, vaulted himself up on the counter and shouted, "175!"

He fell back laughing and darted away into the kitchen.

"I'm sorry, sir, I could just not find a sitter today. Now let me guess: You're a hot man."

Before Jim could stammer, she was sprinkling a handful of hot-sauce packets on his tray. Jim was actually a mild-sauce man, which made him love it even more.

"Is there anything else I can do for you?" she asked.

"Not that I can think of," he said.

It was true. He couldn't think of a thing. He felt that his mind had been washed, dried, fluffed and folded. Jim floated back to a corner booth. The dining room and the world outside it—barely distinct through the current of late afternoon light coming in through the window—relaxed as he did. His combo was exactly the same soft, unctuous consolation it had always been and would be forever.

He did not feel like leaving when he had finished. He bussed his tray and refilled his Wild Cherry Pepsi twice and sat, and he still did not feel like leaving. There was no one looking back at him. No glances wondering what kind of hopeless loser finds a Taco Bell comfortable, or thinking he might be homeless.

On the periphery of his hearing, Gordon murmured a joke and Shaniqua laughed. The hush that followed in the subsequent hours that Jim sat, then slouched, then laid there with his back against the wall, arms on the table and over the back of the seat—felt like a quiet dip in a conversation between him, Gordon, Shaniqua and the Yum! Brands corporation. Jim missed a meeting that afternoon, hanging out in a Taco Bell.

Jim never would have combined the words like that, or said them out loud. Nonetheless it was true. Jim believed in Taco Bell. Always had. And in McDonald's and Burger King and Wendy's and Pizza Hut and KFC and Arthur Treacher's and Nathan's and all their competitors, always and everywhere.

Deep in the flickering ball of Christmas lights that made up the sum total of Jim's existence, three neurons had knotted. One was a half-second memory of his mother holding his hand and opening a Dairy Queen door. The second one glowed blue with 39 years of commercials, playing and promising in an ever lengthening loop. The last held the chemically coded taste of a perfectly salted French fry.

This little lump was the nub of Jim's faith that the McRib sandwich would taste as good as it looked on the commercials; that he deserved a break today; that the 11 herbs and spices represented a genuine mystery; that individual locations were part of something larger than themselves, and that chains had discernable personalities; that the high-school girls running the registers upsold you because they wanted you to get the better deal.

It was a difficult faith to keep when staring down urine-draped toilet seats in anarchic bathrooms and surly 17-year-olds who shouted "Have a nice day" as they looked right through you. It wobbled when he opened his Popeye's bag to find they'd forgotten his biscuits and the only thing he had wanted had been those biscuits. It deserted him entirely after each meal and left him squirming on the toilet at home, feeling like a demon was inflating the spare tire around his waist.

Yet it was never away for more than a few hours. And even while it was gone, the hope that it rested on remained: The hope that somehow these places knew him as well as he knew them. Lolling his head around the dining room it seemed, for the first time, a reasonable hope.

Jim was able to leave only by planning when he'd be back. He didn't want to ruin the experience by getting sick of the food. He decided to come back for lunch the day after next. When he did, he found the doors locked and the lights off. The day after that it had become a Lens Crafters.

Back in his apartment that night, Jim clearly remembered passing the Taco Bell behind the Mr. Subb on Central, but the only explanation that made sense was that he did not actually remember this, and that his Taco Bell was actually inside one of the half-dozen other Albany County Taco Bells he knew. Traffic was light this late. He could check them out and still be back for *SportsCenter*. What snapped Jim away from the nebulous kitchen was not what the officer said, but the officer's laughter.

"Hungry, sir?"

Jim tripped backwards off his toes and tried to stammer out that he was looking for a friend. The cop cut Jim off, to tell him how hilarious he'd been.

"Like a pig on two legs with its snout pressed—"

Laughter was coming out of the cop's nose. When he collected himself, eventually, he made Jim recite the alphabet backwards and left him with a ticket for reckless driving.

Google could only find one record of a Taco Bell on Central Avenue, and it was for a Taco Bell on a Central Avenue in a city in Indiana that Jim had never heard of. He eventually did get an actual person on the line at 1-800-TACO-BELL: a Hindu voice that rounded her vowels into pearls and identified herself as Roxy. Jim explained and Roxy listened so intently, he thought, that when he stopped to breathe he could hear through her, to the tiny sound of phones ringing in the background.

She asked him how he would rate his experience at Taco Bell: poor, fair, good or excellent? Definitely excellent. She quizzed him on cleanliness and customer safety measures. Excellent. Excellent. Excellent. He asked if all of these excellents would mean raises for Gordon and Shaniqua. Roxy dropped away into silence. After a moment, she admitted that her system did not contain the names of individual Taco Bell team members. Nor could she find any Taco Bell locations on Central Avenue in Albany. But his survey participation was very important in improving customer satisfaction throughout all Taco Bell restaurants. If he would provide his e-mail address, Roxy said, she would like to e-mail him a coupon for a free soft or crunchy taco, for his feedback. Jim accepted only reluctantly.

He didn't have any use for it. He went back to the Lens Crafters once. He tried on sunglasses, and tried to think of a reason why they would know anything about the previous tenants, until a woman in white coat asked if she could help him. "Just looking," he mumbled, and hustled out.

On a Saturday, on the desperate chance that Yum! Brands had forced his Taco Bell to convert and relocate, Jim drove two hours to a new KFC in Syracuse and strained to hear an accent over the drive–thru intercom. Peeling away and gunning it out into the wide open range of the weekend afternoon, Jim told himself that these places had been lying to him his whole life. But what was he going to do about it? He had to eat.

A chicken place opened next to Jim's office. He couldn't leave the building without passing it, or the button–sized Mexican woman who stood in front holding out one-dollar–off "Grund Opening" coupons. He took one once and carelessly looked her in her needy eyes. Then he felt obliged to eat their mangy popcorn chicken for lunch every day until a rainy afternoon forced her off the sidewalk, after which point he took to walking on the other side of the street.

No place else stuck. Jim's colon was getting too old for McDonald's more than twice a week. Burger King had gone the way of the buffalo. Arby's was a roast beef novelty act. Subway was a refreshing change of pace. Jim felt healthy just for opening the door. Yet no matter how much rehearsed his order in his head—Italian bread, footlong, Italian sandwich, green peppers, extra olive oil—when he got to the front of the line he always blurted out the sandwich type before the bread, and the kid behind the counter would look at him like he was wearing a unitard. Denny's reminded him how nice it was to be served. At the one on Wolf Road Jim could get a Grand Slam and a coffee, and if they weren't busy, the waitresses would keep refilling him, without attitude, all night. If they were busy, though, they would stick him at a table in the middle of the floor and it would be like eating pancakes in a crowded hallway, and he could be left there dangling over his empty plate for forty-five minutes until they brought him his check.

Rolling out from a Dunkin Donuts lot and onto Madison Ave after dinner one night, Jim's half-full Pepsi tipped out of the cup holder and spilled on his leg. Irritated by the moisture nipping through his jeans, he clenched his tongue against the roof of mouth and tasted the dull fructose sap lingering there. And it just popped into his head: He was tasting the Pepsi through his skin.

He bantered with the idea like it was an absurd and giddy companion. He could turn his new talent in to a county fair freak show act. Or he and the guy who could distinguish between bottles of Coke could form a superhero team and use their powers to solve soft–drink related crimes.

The chance appearance of the memory of the Coke man choked off Jim's good mood. He still didn't believe such powers were possible. He'd seen the inside of a bottling plant on the Discovery Channel once: neatly stacked to the warehouse rafters with stainless steel monoliths hissing and spinning out an immeasurable chain of black bottles. What was ominous about this memory now was that it suddenly came with a fizzling hope that he was wrong, and that each sloshing plastic tub could have more to it than that.

Who was this Coke idiot anyway? A total nut job. A shut–in who assaulted the attention of relatives with preposterous claims. Maybe it was possible that he had, once, gotten a bottle with a half–ounce more corn syrup than usual and being an isolated kook to begin with, had spun out that instant of sensory flux into an ornate delusion, festooning it for the rest of his life with mundane distinctions until it grew to be the only thing that people could remember about him even a few months after he died. Jim was still thinking about this when he blew past the turn for his apartment complex.

And he hadn't entirely squeezed it out of his head by the time he marched into Price Chopper ready to cook for himself. He stumbled early on in the produce department, forcing himself to search for an unintimidating green vegetable until he realized he's been there for twenty minutes, and if he didn't pick up something soon, someone would think he was a retarded employee. He fled the area with a bag of Granny Smith apples. Jim fought the urge to beeline for frozen foods. Things got baffling in the bakery department and he took three redundant loaves of bread. By the dairy section he was in despair. He saw the only thing he could make from the mess he'd gathered were apple sandwiches on paper plates with baking soda on the side. He seized an armload of Hamburger Helper boxes and five pounds of ground beef and kept his head down at checkout.

It turned out great, actually. The slow sound of simmering meat in his long silent kitchen reminded Jim of a crackling fireplace. Chili Cheese, Double Cheeseburger Mac, Cheesy Italian Shells and Cheesy Hashbrown took their places in the rotation. Each tucked an identical warm, saline blanket over Jim's tongue, which juxtaposed perfectly with the sweet bite of the Granny Smiths he cut up. So perfectly, that he was sure he was taking his life in the right direction when he decided to slice the apples directly into the Hamburger Helper. The next night he was at Wendy's.

Jim would have told you that he'd forgotten his Taco Bell right up until he saw the sign. It was almost six. A wall of clouds that had been incipient all day was finally pushing over downtown. The last state workers leaving out North Pearl Street towards 787 flicked their headlights on against the gloaming. Rain was already falling when Jim hurried out of his lawyer's building onto the alley where he'd parked. As he hesitated in the doorway he glanced over and saw a sheet of copy paper taped to the faded-yellow brick office building across the way, with a hand drawn purple arrow pointing to a service door.

It was the particular purpleness of the arrow that drew Jim down a series of cinderblock hallways, to an old marble lobby, to another arrow, pointing up, taped to the desk of a sleeping security guard. He rode the shoebox elevator to every floor and searched. The hallways were over-carpeted and airless. The opaque windows set in the ancient wooden doors looked like they should have had private detectives' names stenciled on them, but had nothing. The only difference on the top floor was that at the end of the last hall there was an aluminum–framed glass panel door pouring out white light. And through it was Gordon, standing square behind the register.

"Our first customer of the day! Welcome!" he called as Jim tentatively made his way to the counter.

Shaniqua appeared from the kitchen with her thumb in an accounting textbook.

"What a treat," she said. "I better plug in the microwave."

Jim wasn't entirely speechless. He could order a number seven combo. He couldn't tell whether either of them remembered him. Shaniqua held a tender, mothering note in her voice as called his number. That could have been the way she always was though. Jim wanted to ask her about what had happened on Central, but not as badly as he thought he would. What he desperately wanted to ask her was how she was, what she was doing with her life, and how the boys were. Of course, if she didn't remember him, this would make him a stalker.

"This is a strange space," is what he managed to get out as she was turning back to the kitchen.

"Yeah, it is. Mr. Abdulkawan, he's the franchisee, you could say he has a different business sense."

The dining room was a mustard yellow box that had until recently been a waiting room in the office of an ancient and lonely doctor. Three booths huddled against the far wall. In front of them a single table tilted on the uneven floor. The only window was only part of a window, in the far corner, halved by the butt end of a hastily thrown-up sheetrock wall. The counter had never been meant for exchanging anything larger than insurance forms. If Gordon was working the register and Shaniqua calling out orders they would be shoulder to shoulder. Just to the right of the door, the hallway to the exam rooms was blocked by a bank of soda dispensers. A universe of incongruities had been miniaturized in here. To Jim, it was majestic.

He took the window booth, knowing that he should have been panicking. As he ate, he reminded himself that this could be a dream and that even if it wasn't, he would have to leave soon and this should terrify him. At the same time his head felt so pleasantly, thickly creamy, like a vat of melted cheese being stirred slowly and rhythmically, that all his efforts at reason dissolved.

He was asleep on his arms before his quesadilla was even out of the wrapper. When he woke, hours later the room was dim, except for a small light in the kitchen they had left on for him, and a Styrofoam doggie-bag box perched by his elbow, with a note taped on:

"The door locks behind you. We open tomorrow morning at 8. ☺"

Jim was back at 7:45. Gordon was already there, scrambling eggs for a special southwest breakfast burrito that wasn't technically on the menu. Jim returned at breakfast—and dinnertime—for weeks. Neither Gordon nor Shaniqua ever mentioned his nap. They remained bafflingly polite. When Jim got sick of tacos they didn't mind that he bought in McDonald's.

The only thing was, the small talk never grew. Jim took comfort in the fact that they weren't any closer to the handful of other customers. From his window booth, Jim saw a young man in a black double-breasted suit attempt to pay for a grilled stuffed burrito with a succession of maxed-out credit cards. He apologized as Gordon handed each one back, confessing first that he wasn't good at juggling so many cards; then that he was a complete and total fraud; and finally, that he was poor.

"No problem, sir. It costs Taco Bell about fifteen cents to make these things," was all Gordon said. Shaniqua handed the man his to-go bag.

Then there was the old harpy. She came in, ordered, then returned her nachos supreme without touching them and sat back in her chair, sideways, waiting for her replacement like a gray flannel idol expecting a sacrifice. And Shaniqua sacrificed: she came out, put the new nachos on the table and kneeled in front of the old woman. She took the old woman's nearly transparent hand in hers and squeezed gently.

"I am so sorry," Shaniqua said. "You need low-fat sour cream. I know how it is. My aunt has high cholesterol, too."

The woman mumbled for a moment and gazed over Shaniqua's shoulder; partly embarrassed by the sincerity, partly stunned, as if she was seeing every eye-rolling salesgirl and non–English proficient gas station attendant she had suffered in her excruciatingly long life forming a line behind Shaniqua, waiting for their turn to apologize. Shaniqua held the woman's hand for ten minutes.

Jim did what he could to pry at the margins of Gordon and Shaniqua's pleasantries. How was Mr. Abdulkawan doing these days? How long had they been at this location? Their customer-service jujitsu was flawless.

"Feels like we've been here forever," Gordon would say and chuckle. "That's the way it is with work, right sir?" All he could find out about Mr. Abdulkawan was that he rarely came by.

Not long after he had decided to stop nursing his curiosity, Jim went for a Pepsi refill on his way out. The plastic nozzle coughed as he poked his cup under it, and what came out was still and bitter. Shaniqua and Gordon were back in the kitchen. Jim didn't feel right bothering them. It stayed broken for weeks.

Gordon was astonished when Jim finally told him. He tipped himself a cup and sipped thoughtfully, swishing and squinting more than he had to.

"I don't know, sir," Gordon shrugged. "Tastes about right to me."

Jim took Gordon's cup and took a swig for himself.

"Are you sure? It's not even carbonated," said Jim.

"I could have Mr. Abdulkawan check the hoses when he comes in."

"But it tastes fine to you as it is right now?"

"It tastes like Pepsi."

Gordon apologized for the difference of opinion. He reached behind the counter and came back with one of the large-size plastic cups. He presented it to Jim.

"For our best customer," said Gordon, tapping his high–beam smile. "We really are sorry for the inconvenience. But consider this good for life. Any beverage. Any time. Complimentary."

Normally he liked these cups, for their durability and how they commemorated meals he would have otherwise forgotten. When he got one of them he always meant to wash it out at home and keep it so eventually he would never have to buy another cup again. Invariably, he only remembered this plan after the cup had been sitting in the car for days and was caked beyond hope with tenacious globules of dried cola. Normally, too, "best customer" would have been the sort of compliment he noticed. Jim took the cup and half–filled it with Sierra Mist, just to be gracious, and left.

He knew that moping for a week and four days was an infantile way of handling it. Exactly how much did he expect from his Taco Bell? Should Gordon and Shaniqua have to wear their hair like him? It made as much sense as expecting them to have the same constellation of taste buds. They would have let him bring his own Pepsi. They would have let him make his own Pepsi in there. When his self-deprecation could make him laugh again he went back to find that it was gone.

It wasn't hard for Jim not to mention his Taco Bell to anyone. He only came close once. Picking at a plate of bourbon chicken in the Colonie Center food court he overheard the wad of teenagers at the table behind him throwing straws at each other and complaining.

Everything here sucked. Cajun Café sucked. Sbarro sucked. That sushi place was grody. One teenager felt like Taco Bell. Another remembered that there was one at the Crossgates food court. They all agreed on the awesomeness of Taco Bell, but, by the time Jim decided to turn around, they were gone too.

Tête-à-Tête
Christina Murphy

Harry Shipley was growing warts.

He had received the power in a special dream.

Now, whenever he concentrated and turned his mind to a silvery haze, he could point his finger and grow a wart on the exact spot the finger indicated.

He was growing his warts everywhere: in the kitchen, on the lamp shades, on the windowsills, the chairs. Warts were in his laundry basket, in the potted plants, on the ceiling, the floor.

Harry was very happy with his warts. They were wonderful company and took a lot less time than a garden. He was most proud of his six-foot wart in the basement, Godzilla, a rose-colored wart that was growing a hair. The hair had started quietly one day when Harry was down in the basement checking on his supply of coal for the winter. When he reached for the light, he noticed a small projectile, much like a blade of silver grass, sticking out of Godzilla's head. The hair grew three feet in two weeks and took on a lustrous, almost iridescent sheen. Harry took very good care of the hair and washed it regularly. One evening he curled the hair with a rolling pin and was very proud when the hair looked like a little silver snake coiled on top of Godzilla's head.

When Harry went down to the basement one night late in the winter, he was stunned by what he saw. The hair had grown to an enormous length and had wrapped itself around Godzilla several times. To his horror, he watched the hair uncoil, stretch out the basement window, and stroke the thigh of the choir mistress of the All Saints Episcopal Church as she walked by.

"Oh my heavens, my God, what was *that?*" he heard her scream as she ran to the back of his house and started pounding on the door.

He raced up the steps and opened the door.

"There's a thing, a monster in your basement, it just... it just reached up and..."

"I'd better go check on it."

He slammed the door and bolted it; then he was in the basement digging around, searching. He found the garden shears and advanced upon the hair, ready to cut it off at the root, but the hair gave off a low, humming sound and turned into a puff of blue smoke. A little man the size of Harry's fist appeared in the smoke. He looked at the garden shears.

"I'd advise against it."

"Why?" Harry asked, holding the garden shears even tighter.

"Because you won't get your wish."

"What wish?"

"I'm a genie, pal. I can make your deepest wish come true."

"How do I know that?"

"Try me. Think of what you want most in life, and I'll give it to you."

Harry considered his desires. He thought he might like a wife, but she might turn into a shrew and make his life miserable. Wealth would be intriguing for awhile, but soon he'd run out of things to buy and be very bored. Physical beauty, maybe, but that would always be more interesting for the people looking at him than it would be for him. Youth and a long life would be good things to have if the world weren't so rotten and getting worse by the minute. The more he thought, the more he was getting stumped and confused, but then he knew what he wanted.

"I want power," he said to the little man who was sitting in the cloud of smoke, his legs crossed, his foot dangling.

"Okay, then Power it is," the genie said, making a puff of smoke appear on the basement floor, out of which stepped a woman about three feet tall with a buttercup-shaped proboscis, large floppy, elephant-like ears, and red eyes that rolled around in her head like pinwheels.

"What's *that?*" Harry said in horror.

"That's Power."

"But *that's* not what I wanted!"

"But it is what you asked for. Always be specific with a genie, pal," the little man said as the puff of smoke he was sitting on got smaller and smaller and disappeared with a pop, leaving only Harry and Godzilla and this strange creature that looked at Harry now with eyes that spun.

"Jesus H. Christ. What am I supposed to do with..."

The creature came over and hugged Harry's leg. He tried to shake her off, pull her free, but he couldn't move her.

He dragged himself up the basement stairs, Power holding on to his leg, and sat down at the kitchen table.

"Get off my leg!"

Power looked up at him, spun her eyes, and made a soft sound like a mechanical purring.

"What a goddamn mess. I could have had wealth, I could have had beauty, and I get this thing, stuck to my leg."

He went into the living room and sat on the sofa. Power scurried up his leg and sat on his lap. The soft mechanical sound became deeper.

He looked at Power. Her eyes were spinning so quickly they seemed to be giving off crimson sparks. Then Power was standing in his lap, hugging his neck.

"Sit down!" Harry said, but Power only hugged him tighter.

Harry contemplated what to do and was stunned when Power kissed his cheek. It was an odd little kiss, what with her proboscis maneuvering into place, but it was very tender. Power put her head on Harry's shoulder and quickly fell asleep. He could tell she was sleeping deeply because of the rhythmic sound she was making, which sounded very much like snoring.

Harry decided to go to sleep himself and carried Power into the bedroom. He placed her on the loveseat by his bed, gently unwrapping her arms from around his neck. Then he got into bed. He had just begun to doze off when he felt Power get into bed beside him and snuggle up against him. Soon Power was snoring again, and Harry fell asleep entranced by the sound and the feel of Power's tiny body against him.

When the morning came, Power was already standing beside the bed when Harry woke up. She put her arms up like she wanted to be carried, so he complied and took her downstairs to the kitchen. He made his breakfast, a wide selection of everything he could find in the house, and ate ravenously. He could not interest her in bacon or eggs, hash browns or grits, but she did unfurl her buttercup proboscis and suck up a biscuit off his plate. Later in the day, he read the sports section of the paper and she watched TV.

This isn't bad at all, he thought to himself. He remembered the tenderness of her snuggling and decided that maybe he hadn't made such a bad choice after all.

When he went to work the next morning, he left Power eating a biscuit and watching *Good Morning America*. He closed the door, content with his choice, and thinking that life with her might be rather pleasant.

When he got home, he was sickened by what he saw. She had rearranged the furniture and stacked up all his warts in a corner. When he found her, she was potting plants in the kitchen. He was triply mad because, in her repotting, she had overlooked one of his favorite pale pink warts, which was now lying on its side in the sink, nearly buried in a mound of dead roots and chunky peat moss.

"Hey, what're you doing? My plants, my furniture? And my warts? They're not happy like this."

He went over to the pile of warts in the corner and began unstacking them. Power came over and put them back. Harry got really mad and grew two butter bean-sized warts on the ceiling. Power wiggled her ears, and the warts changed to cobwebs.

Harry was furious and pointed his finger to grow a wart on Power's nose. Power wiggled her ears and Harry's finger curved back around toward him, and he had to jump out of the way to avoid getting the wart that now grew on the floor between his feet. Power picked up that wart and put it on the pile.

"I'm not going to stand for this, I'm really not!" Harry said. "This is my house," he said, hitting his chest with his thumb, "*mine*, and you're not in charge here, I am. You hear me?"

Power wiggled her ears, and Harry's pants fell to the floor.

That evening was a very unhappy one for Harry. He tried to watch TV, but Power kept changing the channels. He tried to read, but, right as he got to an interesting part in his book, Power made the next two pages disappear. He missed his warts hanging off the light fixtures and growing on the footstools. He didn't like the way Power had rearranged the room. Once while she was in the bathroom he grew a little amber wart on the edge of the coffee table and hoped she wouldn't see it, but she spotted it right away and turned it into a bouquet of flowers.

When Harry left for work in the morning, he thought of never coming home, but where would he go, and what would he do? He knew he had only his house and his belongings, and, as he came home that day, he didn't know what to expect. He wasn't even sure his house would be in the same place he had left it, but when he got home, everything seemed sane and calm and he was greatly relieved. Power was in the kitchen frying some eggs. Harry said hello and went into the living room. He didn't lose his temper until he saw that his furniture was no longer rearranged but gone. In its place was a prissy French Provencal living room suite that nobody could sit on and tapestries hanging from the walls of knights in full armor riding out to war.

Harry stormed into the kitchen, grabbed Power by the shoulders, and began shaking her.

"I don't want any of this stuff in my house, you understand? I want my old furniture back, and I want it back *now!*"

Power did not like being shaken. Harry caught the warning glance but he couldn't stop himself.

"Give me my furniture! Just give me my furniture!"

Power left him his eyes when she turned him into a paperweight. He watched her carry him into the living room and place him on the little writing desk by the door. He glared at her, shot her looks of bloody rage as she sat on the sofa and calmly ate her eggs. When she put on the TV, she turned him around so that all he could see was the wall. He stared at the pocked and grainy surface of the wall and wondered if she would leave him like this forever. He counted nubs on the plaster and plotted revenge. Late in the evening, she turned him around and looked at him. She wiggled her ears and Harry was himself again. He wanted to kill her, but instead told her thank you and went upstairs to his room. Power came up later and lay down beside him. Harry knew it would be futile to try to leave. Power snuggled against him and held him close all night while she slept.

***

Harry went to work and came home for seven days straight and tried not to agitate Power. He didn't want to be a paperweight again. She was better behaved but still she got on his nerves. For one thing, she was learning to speak a few words. *No* was one of her favorites.

"Let's go to the movies." *No.*

"Well, I'm going to the movies." *No.*

"I'm getting hungry. Let's eat." *No.*

"I need some time to myself." *No.*

"I'm going to watch the baseball game." *No.*

"Well, why don't *you* get a job, then?" *No.*

No. No. No. He was sick of it, and he was sick of her. He was sick of the way she unmade and redid the bed every time he made it, sick of the way she rearranged everything in the house to suit her fancy, sick of not having his warts around for company, and sick of being abused at will.

One day when he was eating his lunch at work, he knew he had reached his limit. He had packed a bologna sandwich, some Cheez-Nips, and two Twinkies, and, unbeknownst to him, she had changed his lunch to a tuna fish sandwich, two carrots, and an apple. At the bottom of his lunch box was a note that said, "Eat better." He slammed his lunch box down, punched out, and drove home.

He was so angry he could hardly keep his car in its lane. He gripped the steering wheel and tried to figure out what to do. He knew he could never sneak up on her, she was too clever for that. And catching her while she was asleep wouldn't work, her hearing was too good. Sometimes he felt that she always knew what he was thinking, so he might as well not try to hide it. He figured a split second was all he had. That and a red glass bead he carried in his pocket for good luck.

He came in the back door. She was watching TV. He knew he had to time this perfectly. He stood in front of her and took the bead from his pocket. She was looking at him, watching him carefully, intensely curious about the bead and what Harry might be doing. He ignored her, focused on the bead in his palm, and began getting his finger into position. He knew it would take an infinitesimal fragment of time before she could respond to any action of his by wiggling her ears, and in that tiny moment he could be saved. He continued to look at his palm and pretended to concentrate. He could tell she was getting irritated with him, not knowing what he was doing. When he saw that first shake, that first miniscule wiggle of her ears, he really did concentrate and zapped her one with his precisely pointed finger. There was a shrill noise, a puff of smoke, and then she was a blue-gray wart the size of a golf ball.

"I did it! I did it!" Harry said, jumping up and down. He was laughing and dancing and hugging himself with glee. He turned back to look, just to be sure, and the wart was the size of a softball, then a basketball, then it was a huge dark globe coming toward him. There was a whirring sound, and the globe was spinning and spinning and then exploding into shards of glass that sliced his skin. One piece ripped into his shoulder and sent blood running down his arm and onto the floor. From the blood, hundreds of miniature Powers emerged—coming together and forming an enormous ball of dark glass. The whirring sound began anew, and Power materialized as a massive form.

She came toward Harry and grabbed him with her proboscis, holding him up to her angry red eyes and shaking him hard.

"No," she said. "No!"

Power was holding him so tightly that Harry could feel his heart pounding wildly in his chest. He struggled to get free, and Power threw him down on the floor and into his own blood. Harry felt a searing sensation and watched in horror as his hands turned into blue-gray warts. Only one finger remained on his right hand, and it was pointing right at his heart, ready to zap him as Power looked on.

How to Tell Your Aunt and Uncle You Want to Marry Their Daughter

Kevin Brown

One.

Be prepared to die.

Know it has happened before and for a whole lot less. Understand that what you're asking them to consent to is widely accepted as sick, blasphemous, and, first and worst, politically incorrect. Forget the notion of "blind love" and the inexplicable mysteries of the heart, you're facing scandal here. And do keep in mind her father was a purple-heart recipient after two tours of duty in Vietnam. Don't forget he lost an arm to the elbow doing it.

So to summarize, what you're doing takes lots of balls and lots more stupidity.

Pray you've got the right combination of both.

Two.

On the night this is to go down, their daughter (and since two Tuesdays from last Monday, your fiancée) Devin— WILL. NOT. BE. THERE.

Take a second. Maybe two. Repeat this line. Maybe twice.

Devin will be in the Motel 6 near the State Line, sweating and pacing and gnawing her fingernails to the forearm. In most situations where "young-man-asks-father-for-younger-daughter's-hand-in-marriage," it is beneficial, even wise, for her to be present, for: A.) Emotional, mental, and possibly physical support. And: B.) So they can witness that glazed-over look of love in her eyes.

Here, that's just not going to fly.

Them seeing their daughter wrap her hand around your knee will only crystallize the horror already forming in their minds, and it has nothing to do with love. It has to do with

S

E

X.

Memorize those letters. Now forget them.

Three.

Wear your police uniform. Your shirt and trousers should be crisp and hand-pressed to a pleat. Shoes buffed. Studies have shown an officer's uniform's paramilitary appearance has a strong psychological influence in the minds of civilians. It conveys power and authority, yet safety. But more importantly to you, it tends to curb most illegal and dubious behavior.

Take the police cruiser. Wear your weapon belt.

Think about stopping off for an expensive bottle of wine, but don't. They know you're not a classy wine guy. The small bulb of gut pushing your shirt out shows you're a cheap beer man through and through. Plus, you don't want to give this man and his wife alcohol to wash down what you're about to tell them.

Equation: Alcohol + Incest x Nam Flashbacks = Very Bad Things^2.

Pull up to their house and kill time. When delivering bad news of accidents to unsuspecting parents, police procedure states an officer should turn on his or her flashers and make plenty of noise on the way to the front door. Let them see you, let the images do some of the work so they can ease into the shock of what they're about to hear. So they sort of know what's coming without knowing.

Follow this advice.

Before you ring the doorbell, call Devin and tell her you're about to go in. Say, "I'll call you when it's over." Blow her a kiss through the phone. "It's okay," say. Say, "I loved you."

Take a deep breath, ring the bell, and hope it's not an omen that you said "loved" past perfect, instead of "love" present tense.

Four.

When your aunt lets you in, they know something's up. She puts her hand to her mouth and says, "What's happened?"

Wave your hand and say, "No, no. Nothing's happened." Think about thinking about what happened twice last night and once this morning.

Don't.

Kiss her on the cheek and shake his good hand firm, never breaking eye contact. Show him you're a stand-up guy. Ready to protect and to serve. Not the skinny snot-nosed nephew they've come to know and shrug off.

Take your shoes off at the door. You don't want to stain their carpet. You're already staining enough.

Five.

When they ask if you want some water or a soda, say,
"Please, thank you." Usually, drinking from their cup
would be a negative and metaphorically redundant, but
you'll need something to keep your throat from drying up.
Your voice has to be strong and unwavering. Plus, props
are nice. However, sip it slow. You don't want to have to
piss in the middle of all this.

    "What can we do for you, *officer*?" your aunt says,
smiling that smile she smiles when she doesn't feel like
smiling. She cups her coffee with both hands and leans
forward on the sofa. Your uncle kicks back in his old
recliner and grimaces. Try not to stare at his swollen leg,
where the Agent Orange has turned it blue. To your
dismay, he's drinking from a bottle of Wild Turkey. Notice
the level's below the label.

    Deep breath. Find your center.

    Now.

    Lean forward like her, say, "I'm here to ask
permission to marry Devin," and lean back, lacing your
fingers in your lap.

    Let the silence hang.

Six.

Continue to let the silence hang.

Seven.

Sip your water to wet your lips. Think about speaking.
Decide to wait. Bite down until your jaw pops and angles
off. Feel helium-headed and slimy-palmed, what could

only be either unbridled fear or giddy excitement. Clear your throat and ignore the pearl of sweat sliding over the ridges of your ribs. Stare at your uncle's bottle of liquor. Quiver at the thought of a drink.

Your aunt palms her throat and doesn't blink.

Your uncle takes a drink and doesn't blink.

They stare at each other, speaking but not.

And this is where all the planning and the planning to plan and the planning to plan the plan pays off—you know *exactly* what will happen next, as if you are clairvoyant.

As if you could just see—

Your uncle will throw his head back to toss off the whiskey in a couple pumps of the throat. Your aunt will start to cry and tremble and place the back of her hand to her forehead, then topple down like a dropped dishrag. Your uncle will wiggle and shimmy in his recliner, mumbling, "*Little shit. Little bastard. Little…*" You will hold your hands up to invisibly Etch-A-Sketch explanations that fire off like pistol blasts: "*We love each other. Have for years. She wanted to be here, but was afraid you wouldn't understand…*" Your aunt will howl, "*My baby, my girl, God help her!*" and her eyes will flutter and roll back in her head. And your uncle: "*Cocksucker. Motherfucker. Son of a bitch…*" And you: "*Love knows no bounds. The Blue Bloods kept it in the family. The Greeks were freaks and just look at their legacy…!*" And you'll regret using the word 'freak,' but it'll be too late. Your aunt will twitch and tremor and seizure like boiling water, and your uncle'll finally make it out of the chair. You'll stand to meet him, hand resting on the butt of your firearm. He'll head down the hall, screaming: "*Dick-lick, sperm-spitting, testicle-tasting…*" And you'll come to the conclusion he's not going to grab a wedding gift, so you'll bolt. Out the door, to the police cruiser. In the rearview, he'll burst out, shotgun in one hand, flipper

flipping, limping and screaming under the porch light.
You'll go left at the stop sign and head to the freeway. To
the Motel Six. You'll call Devin and yell: *"Plan B! PlanB!"*
She'll meet you in the parking lot, two suitcases under her
arms. She'll be crying when you leave the cruiser and take
your civilian jeep. You'll head west. Head to Vegas. Get
married in the *WE IN A HURRY* wedding chapel.
Continue on. You'll hit L.A. and Santa Cruz, the sun
glowing. Hit Crescent City and cross the state line into
Oregon, through the walls of redwoods. Stop off at a place
called Coos Bay. You'll both love it and decide to make it
your home. After a year of financial difficulty, you'll get a
job as the local deputy. She'll go back to college. You'll
buy a small house on the beach. Fix it up and make it
"home." Have three beautiful kids. Name them: Kaden,
Alex, and Varian. Kaden and Alex will grow up to be
quarterback brothers in the NFL. Varian will be a District
Attorney with her grandfather's eyes and her
grandmother's sense of melodrama. You and Devin will
sip Mai Tais, then V8, then coffee on the porch, and watch
your grandchildren play in the yard. You'll walk hand-in-
hand along the beach, your hair as white as the sand, and
watch the waves roll and foam around your feet, then slide
silver back into the ocean. And—

"You have our blessing," your aunt says, still
palming her throat.

Blink a few times. Realize where you are. What
you're doing. "I'm sorry?" say. "I what?"

"She said," he says, "go for it. What makes her
happy, makes us happy." He takes a drink. "But you hurt
her, I hurt you. Cop be damned. Nephew double-
damned."

Say, "Yessir." Say, "Understood." Then, pointing at
the bottle, say, "Spare a shot?"

Eight.

Walk out into the dark silence. Look around. Feel what you felt when you saw your first overrated meteor shower. Got laid the first over-hyped time. When the Apocalyptic Armageddon of Y2K finally arrived, and not a damn thing happened.

Walk to your cruiser and get in. Feel the vibration of your cell phone against your leg. See it light up blue inside your pocket.

Devin.

Don't answer.

It rings again.

Still don't answer.

Turn it off. Toss it in the seat.

Drive to the stop sign and look left. See the glowing freeway that meanders and paves off to everywhere else. Stretches out and on to where you will never go. To places and people and things you will never see. Vegas. L.A. and Santa Cruz. Up the coast, where the sun deflates into the ocean. Through the redwoods reaching up and old into infinity. Think about corners you'll never disappear around. Hills you'll never crest. Deputies you'll never be and colleges she won't go back to. Picture the house you won't buy and fix up, and the kids you won't conceive. Sons who won't grow to be quarterbacks. No District Attorney daughter. Mai Tais then V8 then Coffee you'll never drink, your arm around your wife, watching grandchildren play in the yard. Think about the beach you and Devin won't walk hand-in-hand on, the surf you won't see rush white as your hair around your feet and slide metallic back into the ocean. The waves you will never hear, hissing and bursting like plans, like dreams against the jagged rocks.

"Grab some milk!" she shouts.

"There isn't any milk!" the girl frantically replies.

"What do you mean there isn't any milk?!" she yells back.

"I... I don't know," the girl stutters. "There isn't any here. The shelves are empty!"

"Empty? EMPTY?!? What are we going to do?! How are we supposed to dig our way to the surface when the e-vac units arrive? Without milk to fortify our bones, surely we will succumb to the horrors of osteoporosis!"

"Plus, our cereal will be so dry!" the girl adds, wailing, "It will taste terrible!"

The futility of the situation descends upon them like the eye of a hurricane; an unsettling calm that allows them just a breath before destroying it again. It is one of those seconds that seem to last an eternity, caustic and silent, like a river of oil in a sea of vinegar.

"I guess this is it," she says soberly, unzipping her fanny pack and pulling out a clear glass vial. She pops the lid and removes two capsules. "Here, take this pill," she says, handing the girl a dose.

"What is it?" the girl asks.

"Cyanide," she replies.

The girl looks at the small blue pill in her hand. It almost looks like candy. She closes her eyes and exhales dramatically. "I love you, mom," she says.

"I love you too, honey," the mother replies.

They take the pills and, moments later, drop dead in unison.

"What's going on?" I ask O'Donnell, nodding towards the stack of bodies piling up in front of the dairy case. It is only my third day of work at the supermarket and I am not used to these kind of mass suicides yet.

"This isn't typical," O'Donnell says, "They usually just buy the milk and leave. Then again, we usually don't run out of milk, so it's hard to say."

"What's so special about today?" I go.

"Have you been living in a box, man? Take a look outside. It's the Snowpocalypse. The End of the World," his words are remorseful and teary. "If you need to hold me, it's okay," he goes.

"I'll pass for now," I say.

"Suit yourself," O'Donnell shrugs. He curls up in a little ball in the corner and commences crapping himself.

***

Meanwhile, the store manager, Larry Levinworth, is directing the human traffic. He is standing on the conveyer belt of Register 5, holding a shotgun at his hip, looking very manly each time the front door opens and the wind rushes in, blowing his mane of chest hair in all directions. I am struck with the sudden urge to sculpt him out of Ore-Ida instant mashed potatoes, but I brush off the feeling as mild angina.

Shoppers clamour at his feet. Desperately they bleat out their brand-name provisions, hoping a gentle nod of Larry's head could lend a compass to their hectic journey:

"Tropicana orange juice!"

"Quaker Oats oatmeal!"

"Chiquita bananas!"

- and -

"Mott's applesauce. Mott's applesauce! Goddamnit, which aisle is the Mott's applesauce in?!? MOTHERFUCKER, I NEED MY MOTHERFUCKING MOTT'S APPLESAUCE!! BLAUGHHAGDADFDADADFAGIGIGADFIGNHCZ!!!"

Larry puts the rabid patron down with a single shotgun blast to the skull.

At the base of Register 5 is Sandy, the most beautiful of all the checkout girls. Quickly, she scans items, her arms just a blur of color and white noise. Sweat cascades down her milquetoast brow. I could just imagine how good that sweat might taste. Like butterscotch. Or strawberry. Or perhaps shrimp scampi.

A sweet-looking elderly woman stands in front of her.

"Wait, I have a coupon," the elderly woman croaks.

Sandy gives a glance to the amassing line whose vengeful, hate-filled stares prove to her that there is no God.

The old lady hands her the coupon.

"I'm sorry," says Sandy, "But this item is already on sale."

"What are you saying to me?" asks the old lady.

"I'm saying your coupon won't work on this item," Sandy nervously replies.

"Won't... work..." the old lady starts hyperventilating.

"I'm sorry," Sandy meekly says again.

But the old lady doesn't hear her. The top of her skull fissures and splits and out of her wrinkled skin steps a winged beast. The beast screeches. Jars of Smucker's jam and Vlasic pickles shatter, sending razor-sharp projectiles flying through the air. Sandy cowers. The monster opens its jaws and goes for her head. And just as the beast is about to clamp down, greeting Sandy's fragile brain with that final, fatal crunch, an explosion - *BOOM!* - rings out across the sales floor.

Larry stands over her, grinning – the gun still smoking.

***

Fourteen more mother/daughter combinations have killed themselves in front of me. Outside, it continues to snow. I retreat to the stockroom to look for Wayne, the stock guy, who always has a flask of whiskey in his smock pocket.

I find Wayne, piss-drunk, doing donuts on the motorized hydraulic pallet jack. He giggles like a schoolgirl.

"Justin!" shouts Wayne, "You gotta try this!"

"No thanks," I say.

He stops the jack. "What's wrong with you, dude?" he says. "Did someone poop in your coffee this morning?"

"No, nobody pooped in my coffee this morning. I'm just a little worried because I just found out it's the End of the World," I admit.

"*Pshaw*," Wayne waves me off insouciantly, "Let me tell you the secret to life. You can't let the little things get you down. Every day is the End of the World. You just never noticed before."

"I guess," I say.

"Anyway," Wayne says, "I know something that's going to cheer you up."

"Uh, okay," I go, "But if you about to pull your weiner out again, I'm seriously going to hit you."

Wayne puts his weiner away. He places his arm around my shoulder and whispers in my ear, "I know where to find some milk."

I look at him in disbelief. "You lie!" I shout.

"*Shhh*!" he goes, "If Larry finds out I've been stashing it, there's no doubt he'll fire me... *from a cannon*! No joke. I've seen him do it."

"Take me to it," I tell Wayne.

He looks over his shoulder to make sure we're not being followed/wire-tapped/infiltrated and motions for me to follow him.

***

Larry Levinworth has placed a leash around Sandy's neck. She is in her bra and panties. Larry wears a Burger King paper crown and has declared himself the official King of the Universe. He confidently pulls Sandy around the supermarket. She follows obediently on her hands and knees, wrist-deep in the slush that coats the floor. A few customers have taken to worshipping Larry. They erect a shrine to him out of Bumblebee Tuna and Green Giant vegetable cans. They burn copies of *Us Weekly* at its base to appease their Lord. Larry nods with approval.

***

In the back, Wayne leads me to a mountain of Kraft Yellow American cheese, stacked up to the ceiling. He points to it. Apprehensively, I begin removing bricks until, at the mountain's center, I unearth the much lauded Last Gallon of Milk.

The expiration date on it reads 1983 and it's warm. Very warm. I hold the Milk in my hands like the last precious relic of some forgotten culture.

"How?" I ask in awe.

"I've been saving it for a rainy day," he says, "Or, as the case may be, a snowy day."

"We have to tell O'Donnell," I tell him.

Wayne shakes his head in agreement.

We head back onto the sales floor. "O'Donnell," I call out. My voice battles the patron's screams and satellite muzak to be heard. O'Donnell looks up from his fetal position. I wave the Milk in my hand. His ruby-red face lights up as a devilish smile bisects his grapefruit – the fabled Milk of Ages; it's here, and it's *real!* We've all heard the stories, passed down from generation to generation – for it has been foretold, one day a Milk will come, unlike no others, it ushers with it the dawning of a New Era – and it is then, on that day of Final Judgement, the sinners and saints shall ascend to their thrones and each soul, large and small, shall know what it has done. We thought it the stuff of fairy tales, Sunday schools, and paranoid delusional internet chatrooms. But as sure as I hold this Milk here in my hand, every prophetic word of those childhood stories come flooding back to the banks of our collective memory:

I feel like Noah. And this Milk is my Ark.

O'Donnell stands up and starts running in our direction when suddenly a rouge cantaloupe rockets past us. It hits the wall next to O'Donnell and explodes. He is struck by the shrapnel.

"My eyes! My eyes!" O'Donnell screams, "There's citric acid in them." He collapses onto the floor.

"Don't worry O'Donnell, I'll save you!" I shout.

"Justin, don't!" yells Wayne, but it's too late. I grab a Boar's Head Genoa hard salami from behind the deli counter and swashbuckle my way over to O'Donnell. He lays there paralyzed, bleeding, smelling like a fruit salad. He coughs.

"It hurts," he strains, "Oh God, it hurts!" His voice weak and far away. "I don't think I'm going to make it."

"Don't say that, O'Donnell," I say, the tears welling

up.

"I'm so cold," he whispers.

"Well, we are in Frozen Foods," I tell him.

"Just promise me one thing," he goes.

"Anything," I tell him.

"Just protect that Milk. No matter what, protect the Milk. I'd like to believe that somewhere – out there – there's a place with no snow. I want you to take the Milk to that place, Justin. Promise me you'll do that."

"I promise," I softly say, "I promise."

His eyes go white. His muscles fall limp. One last bowel movement fills his khakis and he dies. I close my eyes and whisper a prayer. A few customers shove me out of the way and tear into his stomach, foraging through his intestines for what little crumbs of Planter's peanuts they could find, undigested, inside.

***

Outside, snowflakes the size of footballs fall. They pile up quickly. At least four feet has fallen already and the dark, cloudy, billowing skies show no signs of respite. Eddie, the cart boy, tells us he spotted some polar bears in the parking lot. They were making love to SUVs. The radio reports that an emergency meeting of the House of Representatives to discuss possible evacuation procedures had quickly devolved into a massive orgy/battle royale. The vote is split evenly along party lines. There is no help coming.

We are on our own.

***

Larry is in his office, reviewing the security footage. Sandy does a sexy dance nearby. She dances and cries and her tears turn Larry on, but he is too enthralled by the images on-screen to pay any attention to her or her perfectly proportioned ass.

Larry sees me retreating from O'Donnell's expired corpse. He sees the Milk in my hand. A sinister smirk crawls all over his lips. He grabs his shotgun, throws the leash on Sandy, and heads back to the sales floor.

***

Wayne and I reconvene in Aisle 5.

"What's the plan, then?" I ask.

"Beats me," Wayne concedes. He pulls out the flask and takes a sip.

The florescent lights overhead start to flicker. The muzak is interrupted by the foreboding wail of untuned violins. At the end of the aisle stands Larry, as tall and as granite as the blotted out sun. He is backlit by a red glow emanating from the register's scanners. He shadow sprawls out across the floor, ending at our feet.

A legion of shoppers gather behind him. They are people from all walks of life – teachers, policemen, priests and doctors. Larry demonstrates their collective power by having them sing a few bars of The Oscar Meyer Weiner Song.

"What the fuck?" Wayne says to me, "What is happening to them?"

"I don't know," I reply.

"It's like they've been brainwashed or something," he says.

"Perhaps it's all the years of subliminal messaging that the advertising industry has shoved down our throats," I say, "All the commercial jingles and billboard salvation; all the pressure and speed of our capitalist culture – it's like they've been turned into..."

"Zombies!" Wayne finishes my thought.

Larry points towards us. Without question, the zombies charge.

"Run!" shouts Wayne.

We run from the horde, throwing anything we could find behind us to impede their advance: Butterball turkeys, Charmin toilet paper, Crest toothpaste, Coca-Cola Classic. The products are consumed in their wake; their progress never slowing.

"What are we going to do?" huffs Wayne, his voice trembling with fear.

"Over here!" I point. We pull a sharp right and duck into the stockroom. Wayne continues running, but I stop.

"Come on!" he shouts, "They're coming! They're coming!"

"No," I say defiantly.

"No?!" he gasps, "Are you mad?"

"Perhaps I am," I go, "But I'm tired of it. I'm tired of running. It's this place – it's changed us. Just look at 'em out there. We've been seduced by its convenience. We've let it subvert us, homogenize us, package us and resell us. But underneath its trusty, brand-name facade, it's decaying, quickly, right in our hands. Well no more, I say! This is my food! And my store! And my Milk! And my life! And I say it's time we fought back!"

***

A display for Chips Ahoy! has distracted the horde for the moment. The sale is too good to pass up. Ravenously, they tear at the packages of cookies. The violence of it is enough to damn any Keebler elf to an eternity of nightmares.

"This is our chance," I whisper to Wayne, peering through the stockroom window, "Are you ready?"

"Ready," says Wayne.

And I scream:

"CHARGE!"

We come roaring out to the stockroom on top of the
motorized hydraulic pallet jack. Wayne pilots us straight
into the mob. The Chips Ahoy! display tips over and
flattens a few of them. The rest claw at us. One of them
rips off my shoe. "Sweet, Nike's!" the zombie says. Kicking
free, I stand up on the jack and reach into the fanny pack
around my waist. Grabbing a handful of coupons, I toss
them into the air. Like ticker-tape the coupons rain down
on the crowd and their attention quickly turns to the
savings:

"That one's mine! I had it in my hand!"
"No you didn't."
"Yes I did."
"Fuck off, cocksucker!"
"You fuck off!"
"Give me my damn coupon!"

Their verbal blows quickly turn physical as the petty
name-calling segues into fisticuffs. Wayne pulls the pallet
jack through to the other side as the horde of zombies start
mobilizing into several armies. Things soon escalate into a
full-blown nuclear arms race. All factions of the crowd
have their own atomic warheads:

"Give me my coupon!"
"Never surrender!"
Veni vidi vici, asshat!
Ba-da-da-da-DA, I'm lovin' it!

The nukes are launched. They explode in a
maelstrom of untold devastation, the likes of which Aisle 9
has never seen. Splattered guts drip from ceiling tiles and
shelving units. Umberto, the janitor, comes out, puts a
WET FLOOR sign down, and retreats back to his closet
apartment.

Wayne and I watch from the end of the aisle.

"We did it!" says Wayne.

"Not quite yet," I gravely reply.

***

We pull the pallet jack around to where Larry is standing. Wayne revs the engine. Larry lowers his head, curling his eyebrows into malevolent arches. His face looks like neo-gothic architecture; stone-cold bloodlust fuels his armada. Sandy can only watch, tea-saucer eyed, as Wayne hits the gas and we speed towards them.

Larry lifts the shotgun like it were a part of his own arm, so versed is he with his weapon that if he weren't trying to kill me with it, I'd think it were poetry. Wayne squeezes the throttle until his fingernails crumble and

* BOOM! *

the shotgun sings as we slam into them. The pallet jack careens wildly out of control. We crash through the giant, plate-glass window at the front of the store and all four of us are tossed outside, into the Snowpocalypse.

***

It is minus 40 degrees outside. Sandy's teeth chatter and her nipples go hard and I can't help but look and become slightly aroused. Wayne has been thrown into a snow drift. He lays motionless. I stumble over to him. "Get up," I say, kicking his leg. No response. "Wayne?" I kneel down and shake him harder. He rolls over and where his face used to be is a gaping, bloody hole. Wayne is dead. I want to cry but my tears turn to ice cubes before they can leave my eyes. I exhale a solemn breath. Gently, I pull the flask out of his smock pocket and pour a final sip down his shattered jaw. "Goodbye friend," I say as the snow starts to bury him.

I am overcome with emotions; so fast they surge inside me I only have time to name them before they're gone:

Anger.

Sorrow.

Hopelessness.

Desperation.

Larry is hurt, but he's still breathing. I squint in his direction until one final emotion, the only emotion, solidifies in my soul:

Revenge.

He is on all fours. The blood leaking from his nose paints the ground beneath him psychedelic. "I admire your spunk," Larry says, getting to his knees, "But I hope you realize, it's all useless. You're too late. One man can't make a difference. It's the End of the World. Nothing you're going to do is going to change that."

"That may be," I say, "But you're forgetting one very important thing..."

"Oh yeah? What's that?" scoffs Larry.

"I'm drinking Milk," I say, "And it does a body good." I pop the lid of the warm, decades-expired Last Gallon of Milk, bring it to my lips and start chugging.

My entire body shakes. My stomach turns. I have a bout of diarrhea. And then I grow. My clothes tear off and fall to shreds as swollen, oily muscles canvas my torso. I gain height until I'm 10 feet, 20 feet, 30 feet tall! Larry is taken back a moment, but soon regains his composure and begins unloading round after round from his shotgun. The bullets have no effect on me. They just bounce off my rocky skin and disappear into the blizzard. A wave of terror washes over him. He feebly drops the gun and looks up at me, agape and helpless.

"One man might not make a difference," I boom, my voice so loud and deep it causes avalanches to fall all around us, "But he can sure try, can't he?"

And I step on him.

***

I pick up Sandy and place her on my shoulder. Larry is just a red stain on the pavement. The polar bears and SUVs pick at his remains. I smile triumphantly.

***

I begin walking. The snow continues to fall. Even at 30 feet tall, it is still up to my knees. Sandy clutches onto my back hair. The wind is unforgiving. Sandy scrambles up to my collar and clings onto my ear.

"Justin," she says, her sweet voice desperate, small, and afraid, "Where are we going?"

I look out to the distance. Nothing but white in every direction. All is silent, cold, and lifeless.

"I don't know," I tell her.

And off we go.

English Degree
Ryan Werner

I wrote the script for *A Midsummer's Wet Dream* a week after I got fired from the gas station and a month before I graduated college. I got drunk and sent it to the first adult video company that came up on the internet. Two weeks later I got a check for $175. The day before I graduated college, I got a copy in the mail. I applied at the Adult Warehouse in the next town over and got the job. Graveyard shift.

The clientele were nice. Not in the same ways that a glass of water or a nap are nice, but in the sorts of ways that make them socially upstanding within the context of a store that sells dildos. Virtuous people were everywhere, and I'd take notes on the inside of cigarette cartons as Ms. Asian-Woman-Buying-Imitation-Astro-Glide-In-Bulk told me what makes her feel sexy. She'd leave knowing that it's all for her when the typically demure Ishokino turns to the strong American Buck in *Cumzilla* and says, "Bring your white to my face." My parents told everyone I was in the self-esteem business.

I eventually quit and moved to L.A. Lots of people do it, I realize that, but most of them end up involved with sex on tape only after trying to be in the real movies or on television. I just wanted to see how many different ways I could sneak twenty minutes of story between two hours of fucking. I did the parody circuit at first: *Men In Black Men, Fellatio Gump, Schindler's Lust*. I did *Gummed With the Wind* and *Jurassic Pork* for the nursing home crowd. The studios kept buying. I was doubling up on my student loan payments. I bet they don't teach how to write a cumshot in MFA workshops. Not on purpose, anyways.

Fucktasia moved me away from just writing. I wasn't producing with names or anything—just amateurs who wanted to take a chance—but I was producing. I got calls from studios wanting me to come in and tell them how to shoot the reverse-cowgirl position. I even kept getting calls from home, mainly curious ones that stopped more than they ended.

"Are you eating well?"

"Yeah, Mom. One of the girls made me chili the other day."

My parents have an old phone, and I could hear Mom twist the cord around her finger.

"Is she clean?"

"Well, she didn't make it with her cunt, if that's what you mean."

She handed the phone off to Dad, and only when she was out of the room did I say, "Hey Dad, did you see *Fucktasia*?" But I know they don't care about that sort of thing. The sex, maybe, but not the craft. Most people are like that. Consciously, at least. If someone happened to look, he could see the wrench as Chekhov's gun in *Ballcock* or hear Carver's dialogue in the Vixen Vampire series. When the storm hit the dejected leading man right before the three-way in *Mother Nature's Muddy Fields*, he could see *King Lear*'s pathetic fallacy, and know.

A Parking Space Fit for an Elephant
Stephen Schwegler

Henry Theat pulled into the Church Street parking garage and made his way up to the top floor. Finally finding a spot, he pulled in, put his car in Park, grabbed his briefcase, and walked hurriedly to the elevator.

As the doors were closing he could have sworn it looked like he had parked next to an elephant.

After crossing the street to get to his building, Henry entered into his second elevator of the morning. The music sounded different than usual. He couldn't quite figure out the song, but he knew he had heard it before.

When he got to the sixth floor, Henry exited the elevator and walked toward the front doors of his office. The familiar text on the door had been scraped off.

"Hello?" he said, slowly pushing them open. "Cheryl?"

Cheryl, the receptionist, did not respond. Largely because she wasn't there.

She must be on vacation.

Henry made his way to his cubicle without seeing another employee.

Or maybe it's Saturday?

"Hello?"

No one answered.

Am I... early somehow?

Henry noticed something sitting in his chair. It looked to be a pie tin with some crust remaining.

Someone baked me a pie?

He removed his coat, put down his briefcase, tossed the tin in the garbage, took a seat at his desk and turned on his computer in a single continuous motion. As the decade-old PC booted up, Henry heard shuffling and squeaking coming from the other side of the cubical wall. Curious, he stood on the desk to look over the divider. He was promptly sprayed in the face with seltzer water.

Henry fell backwards into his chair and was immediately beset by a gaggle of clowns. One spun him around while the others sprayed him with more seltzer. Then, without warning, they stopped and scattered.

Henry took this opportunity to make a break for the bathroom.

That's when the floor started shaking.

With each step Henry took the vibrations seemed to be getting more and more violent. Closing in on the bathroom, he lost his balance, falling against the wall.

Just a few more feet...

Regaining his footing, he prepared to make a mad, final dash for the bathroom... and then the rumbling stopped.

Henry jumped at the chance, sprinting down the hallway. He turned the corner and collided with a very large object right next to the bathroom door. A very, very large object. A very, very large, grey, wrinkly object.

Henry Theat ran into an elephant.

On top of the behemoth was a clown holding onto a saddle with one hand. The other hand was tucked behind his back. Henry stared into the clown's eyes, moving slowly towards the restroom entrance, back against the wall. He opened the door quietly, trying not to startle the massive creature in front of him. Still staring down the clown, Henry slipped into the bathroom and immediately locked the door.

Henry walked to the counter, placed his hands astride the sink, and took the deepest breath of this life.

As Henry, still soaked with seltzer, positioned himself awkwardly in front of the air-dryer, the door to the single stall in the bathroom began to creak open.

"Holy shit!" said an incredibly relieved coworker. "Henry, it's you!"

"Noel!" replied Henry. "What's going on out there?"

"I have no idea. I came into the building, took the elevator up and…"

"Wait. You took the elevator too? Did you notice anything strange about the music playing in it?"

"Yeah," replied Noel. "It was circus music. Damn that tune!"

"Right? It's always bothered me."

"Seriously. Anyway, I eventually made it into the office and saw a crap load of clowns. Like a huge crap load. Being terrified of clowns I decided to seek refuge in the can."

"Did you see the elephant out there?"

"The wha?"

"The elephant."

"No. No, I did not."

"It's right outside the door," said Henry, indicating the way with his thumb. "Got a clown riding him."

"Jesus."

"Yeah, it was a little frightening. The elephant seemed cool enough, but I don't trust that clown."

"Well, that does it," said Noel. "I'm never leaving. You think I'll be able to live on toilet paper for, say, another fifty years or so?"

"I'm going to go with a no on this one, Noel. I don't know how that thing even got in here. It wouldn't have fit through the door."

"Listen, if we could just stop talking about it that would be great. Maybe we should think of a way out of here since you're all anti me staying here and eating paper to survive."

"Escape would be good," said Henry. "Seeing as we're both terrified of clowns, though, this will be exceedingly difficult."

"Again, I'm fine with staying here. I'll take my chances."

"Maybe we can break down the wall over there. I think that wall is shared with the women's room."

"You may be right. There could be more toilet paper in there. Maybe even some paper towels! You only have to eat half as many of those to be full."

"But..."

"Ha! Butt."

"... what if there's a clown in there?" continued Henry.

"Oh, man, you're probably right," said Noel. "We're doomed!"

"Hold on, hold on," replied Henry, putting up his hands. "No sense getting all worked up if there's nothing in there. These walls are paper thin. I'll just press my ear against it and see if I can hear anything."

Henry did just that. He placed his head against the wall desperately trying to hear anything that could be construed as clown-like.

And he did.

A squeak.

Henry jumped back in fear and scrambled towards the bathroom door, grabbing the garbage can along the way and barricading the entrance.

"What did you hear?" asked Noel.

Henry, hyperventilating, responded, "Squeaky... shoe... or... nose..."

"Oh God, oh God, oh God!"

"We're fucked, man. Totally fucked. They're everywhere."

Just then someone knocked on the door.

Henry and Noel didn't make a sound.

There was another set of knocks, slightly harder.

The men still didn't make a sound.

A third round of knocks, barely audible.

Noel walked up to the door, leaning over the receptacle. He took a moment to calm himself and said, weakly, "Occupied."

From the other side of the door came, "Ha ha ha ha ha HA HA HAHAHA!"

Noel nearly fell backward at the sound. He staggered toward the back wall, clutching at Henry and trying to hide behind him.

"Fuck fuck fuck fuckity fuck fuck," said a completely panicked and frantic Noel.

"They're going to kill us, aren't they?"

"Henry, I think we're boned."

"No," said Henry. "I'm not giving up that easily. Here's the plan: We make a run for it."

"Not happening."

"Dammit, Noel, we can make it! There's not that much room out there. That elephant has no chance of reaching top speed. We'd be long gone."

"I don't know, man. I don't know."

"Listen. We'll take some rolls of toilet paper as ammo and just run. We run like hell."

"Okay," said Noel, taking a deep breath. "Let's do it. I'm in."

Henry and Noel outfitted themselves with as many rolls of bathroom tissue as they could carry and stuff into their pants. They moved the garbage can away from the door, took deep breaths, and nodded at one another.

Henry knocked open the door and ran. Noel followed close behind.

Henry sprinted past the elephant and across the office floor. He could see the exit. He also remembered it was chilly and he might need his coat.

Henry broke to the left, running down one of the rows toward his cubicle. Noel, however, did not. When Henry emerged on the other end of the cubicle canyon, he looked around and realized that he had lost Noel.

"Noel! Where are you?"

"I'm—" called out Noel weakly.

"Noel!"

Henry could hear muffled screams coming from the other row of cubicles. Then he heard the seltzer. So much seltzer.

"Noel!"

Henry ran over to save him.

"Get off of him you sick bastards!" yelled Henry, ready to take them all on.

But there was only one clown.
It was lying on the ground, shaking and soaking wet. Slowly, it stood up. Hunched forward, its neck craned to one side. It began shuffling, stumbling, toward Henry. The clown corrected its posture, seemingly with difficulty, but with a smile on its face all the same. Grinning from ear to ear it took another step toward Henry.

"Want to smell my flower?" asked the clown.

"Noel?"

"Want to smell my flower?"

"I should probably go..."

"Want to smell my flower?"

Henry ran. He ran faster than he ever had before. Then he got to the elevator and waited. Then he ran into the elevator.

After six floors of ear-splitting circus music the doors opened into the lobby. Henry stumbled backwards. There were clowns. Dozens of clowns. Just milling about. Henry walked through them carefully, slowly, a fake smile on his face, until he was on the street.

The clowns were everywhere.

The elevator of the Church Street parking garage was playing the same music as the one in Henry's building, but it wasn't nearly as loud. Henry exited onto the top floor and saw the elephant.

I guess it's not the same elephant that was in the office after all.

He shrugged and walked toward it.

Could've sworn I parked on this side of it, though.

Then he saw it.

Henry fell to his knees.

The elephant was sitting on his car.

"No, no, no, no, no!" screamed Henry.

Behind him, the elevator began its return to the ground floor.

Henry walked to the edge of the parking structure. He put his hands on the concrete ledge and looked out at the city trying to think of what to do next.

Then he heard the elevator come back up.

Henry turned to find Noel standing in front of the elevator, still smiling, still dressed as a clown. Henry walked over to him.

"Noel, are you okay?"

Noel didn't say a word.

"Do you need help?"

Noel's smile cracked slightly. He lowered his head.

"Yes, Noel?" asked Henry.

Slowly Noel lifted his head, looked into Henry's eyes and said, grinning, "Want to smell my flower?"

Henry sighed and said, "Sure, Noel. Sure."

Mendelssohn Hinkle's One Thing
Jonathan H. Roberts

Much to his parents' disappointment, Mendelssohn Hinkle had no interest in music. He started piano lessons at the age of four, but never developed as a player; in fact, his teacher would often remind him that he was the worst student she'd ever had, lacking the talent that even a monkey possesses. To emphasize this insult, she purchased a chimpanzee and would teach it during Mendelssohn's lessons, forcing him to turn pages for the albino chimp, which she named Alabaster. The ape progressed amazingly well, though he would only play if Mendelssohn was there.

***

While his parents were disheartened by Mendelssohn's musical disinclinations, his grandfather couldn't have been more pleased. Having been the star quarterback at Victory High School in his day, Artimus Hinkle was eager to introduce his grandson to the splendor and glory of organized sport. When try-outs arrived for the youth football league, Artimus took Mendelssohn to watch, and from the sidelines they observed as children were ushered onto the field by proud, hopeful parents, most of them shouting advice as their visibly-shaken little ones joined the herd.

The coaches began calling out names from a clipboard, starting with Philip Hampton, a classmate of Mendelssohn's in Mrs. Strebor's fifth-grade room at Openheyer Elementary School. Mendelssohn watched Philip sprint to the fifty; he was a strong stump of a boy—stocky but quick—and often angry. Philip thought it was ridiculous that Mendelssohn should be named Mendelssohn, and reminded him of this frequently.

"Men... Men-dell... uh... Hinkle! Where's Hinkle?" one coach shouted.

Mendelssohn turned a worried expression toward his grandfather, who simply extended his arms and said, "Surprise!"

"I've never played football, Grandpa."

"It doesn't matter, my boy. It's in your blood."

Mendelssohn climbed down from the bleachers and walked to the field. He looked at the other boys, all of them in sweats and jerseys, and glanced down at the sweater and jeans he was wearing. It was a cool day, and he hadn't dressed to play. He walked as quickly as he could, but when the coach spotted him, he laughed and shouted: "Come on, Mindy!" The other boys began to murmur and laugh. Artimus, who had never so much as thrown a ball with his grandson, watched in horror as his blood proved inadequate to make up for Mendelssohn's complete lack of coordination and physical prowess. The boy could not throw or catch or run or block or cover or tackle. All he could do was stare at the sidelines, just far enough away so that he couldn't make out the look of disgust on his grandfather's face.

Back in the car, covered in mud and bruises, Mendelssohn inspected the tears in his favorite sweater.

"I wish you hadn't put my name in, Grandpa."

The old man sighed. "Me, too."

In school the next day some of the boys spread the news about Mendelssohn's hilarious attempt to be an athlete, and noted that in the future he really ought to be called Mindy. Mrs. Strebor, a stern woman of Slovakian descent, repeatedly told the class not to tease Mendelssohn, reminding them that the shame he felt for failing was difficult enough to deal with, and they should pity rather than persecute. Despite this, she also began calling him Mindy.

The bell rang for morning recess, and as Mendelssohn was pulling his coat down from the peg, Mrs. Strebor called to him, "Mindy, could you stay in here a minute please?" A few giggles from the last stragglers in the room, and he and his teacher were alone. Mendelssohn walked over to her desk, still trying to get his arm through the sleeve of his coat, and asked:

"Yes, Mrs. Strebor?"

"I would like you to stay after school today."

"Am I in trouble?"

The woman smiled, warming as much as she could, and her black, bushy eyebrows arched slightly until they met in the center of her forehead to produce a furry frown. "No, Mindy," she said. "I just want to help you."

"With what?"

"I want to try to find something you're good at."

"Oh. Umm... thank you."

"So you can stay after today?"

Mendelssohn nodded, but then remembered: "Oh, wait. I have piano after school today."

"I didn't know you played piano. So you do have a talent."

He shook his head. "I'm... really awful."

"Well, we're all our own worst critic."

MENDELSSOHN HINKLE'S ONE THING - 131

"No, that's what my teacher tells me."

"Oh." Mrs. Strebor considered that for a moment and said, "Well, I'm sure she knows what she's talking about. Tomorrow then?"

"Okay."

"Great. And don't worry. Everyone has at least one thing they're good at, Mindy."

He nodded and turned to leave. Looking back, he said, "Uh, could you not call me Mindy, please?"

"Oh, I didn't even notice I was doing it. It will never happen again."

But it would.

***

At his lesson that afternoon Mendelssohn found himself once again on the bench beside Alabaster, listening to the chimp play through some of Bach's *Inventions*. Though the time spent there was boring and a bit degrading, Mendelssohn couldn't help but be impressed by the musical proclivities of the ape.

"That's very good, Alabaster! Fingertips, fingertips!" were the offerings drifting in from the other room, where Mendelssohn's "teacher" was stretched out on the sofa with a sleep mask blanketing her eyes.

Alabaster reached the end of the piece, swelling beautifully and then subsiding. He left his hands hovering above the keyboard for a few seconds, and then let them fall gracefully to the bench. After taking a deep breath, he leapt atop the piano and began to clap his hands and hoot excitedly. Mendelssohn patted the chimp's foot.

"That was great, Alabaster."

Alabaster jumped back down to the bench and put his arm around Mendelssohn. He petted the boy's head with his other hand and released a series of soft coos as he deposited several moist kisses on Mendelssohn's cheek. Mendelssohn nodded, not entirely sure what he was agreeing with, and stared into Alabaster's dull, cranberry eyes.

"I don't know," Mendelssohn mumbled. The ape blinked and hugged him.

From the other room: "The Allegro, please! Mendelssohn, have him play the Allegro!"

Then, mumbling, the teacher added, "Stupid monkey never listens to me."

Without a word, Mendelssohn placed the requested piece on the stand and nodded to Alabaster, who cracked his knuckles and began.

***

Artimus Hinkle was at dinner that night. A widower, he came over at least twice a week, and each time he would re-live some glorious moment from his high school career and berate his son for being "one of those music people." His son would then ask what harm there was in music, at which point Artimus would give what he thought was a subtle gesture indicating that Mendelssohn embodied everything that was wrong with music.

"He's not even in the band," his father would say.

"He will be," was always Artimus's answer, at which point Mendelssohn's mother would roll her eyes and say she doubted it. Once this ritualistic conversation was over, there would be a few tense minutes passed in silence, and then Artimus would remember some last tag to the story he had told earlier—an extra point he'd forgotten to kick—and Mendelssohn's father would find a way to segue from this to current events or weather or local people who had died. The meal would then peter out in a trickle of inane chitchat.

Tonight, however, Mendelssohn found himself in a funny mood. He wasn't prone to funny moods, and was as surprised as anyone when he told his grandfather they had already heard the story he was telling at least two hundred times.

"Excuse me?" Artimus said.

"It went into overtime, you ran the last touchdown in yourself, and that's when you learned you can't depend on other people, even if they're on your team," Mendelssohn recited. "You've told this story before, Grandpa. A lot."

Indignation climbed onto Artimus Hinkle's face and settled there.

"Well, I'm very sorry. Perhaps you have a story you'd like to tell?"

"No. I just thought maybe you could tell a different one."

"Okay. How about the one where you went out for the football team? Would you like to hear that one, *Mindy*?"

Mendelssohn's mother sat up, saying, "What are you talking about?"

"I didn't know you went out for the football team," his father said.

"I didn't," was Mendelssohn's reply.

"That's not how I remember it," Artimus said smugly.

Mendelssohn went red.

"That's because you don't remember anything unless it happened to *you* sixty years ago!"

"Mendelssohn!" his father barked.

"I can't believe this!" Artimus roared. "Who do you think you're talking to, huh? I'm the only Hinkle who ever amounted to anything!"

"What?" Mendelssohn's father snapped, forgetting his son's indiscretion. "You played *high school football*, Dad! That's it. Then you worked in a bagel factory for forty years. I at least went to college."

"Oh, so this is where Mindy's attitude is coming from, is it?" Artimus bellowed. "*You're* loading his head with these ideas, are you?"

"*Why do you keep calling my son Mindy?!*"

Mendelssohn left the table as the screams of his father and grandfather escalated. Though much of their argument pertained to him, his absence went unnoticed.

***

Mendelssohn slipped out the back door and into the coolness of the night. He walked down the street, his hands stuffed deep in his pockets, trying to decide if he should be feeling guilty for snapping at his grandfather. He just didn't care about being an athlete or a musician or anything else. Year after year, teacher after teacher, everyone was determined to help him find that special gift that people are born with. The question came repeatedly: "What do you want to be?" And "Mendelssohn" was never an acceptable answer.

"That's who you are, not what you are."

To a ten-year-old mind, it wasn't clear why people had to identify themselves by their accomplishments rather than their nature. That kind of ambition has no inherent appeal to boys who have yet to become men and thus lose the capacity for contentedness.

So Mendelssohn walked along deep in thought, not even hearing the other boys playing in a yard somewhere just out of sight, laughing and tackling each other in the crisp, night air, puffing out their breath while pretending to be smoking cigarettes. He didn't notice them until a football connected with the side of his head with an accuracy too good to have been a mistake. He stumbled to his side, fell to his knees, groping at his right ear and feeling something warm and wet there that could only be blood. He could taste the irony traces of it in his mouth, too, and was vaguely aware he had bitten his tongue.

"Mindy!" came the call, and it was answered by a chorus of laughter.

Mendelssohn fought to get up, but found he had little balance, and teetered back to the ground instantly. This drew another laugh from his audience, and soon he could hear the boys stampeding toward him.

"Mindy, Mindy!"

As he lay on the ground, Mendelssohn waited for the jokes to conclude and the crowd to disperse, but the entire neighborhood seemed to be in a funny mood that night. Another ball smacked his back with a crack like splitting wood. The pain was sharp, and he could feel a welt begin to rise immediately. Instinctively, he rolled and contorted, a hand flying to inspect his back as he struggled to his feet. He caught a blur out of the corner of his eye just before Philip Hampton collided with him, throwing him four feet through the air and back to the ground.

"Hey, Mindy!" he shouted.

Mendelssohn was quicker now, his adrenaline pumping hot, and he was on his feet, assessing the situation.

There were five of them.

Philip was the closest, but Peter and Evan Baker were closing in quickly: identical twins alike in almost every way, though it was debatable which was meaner. Just behind them came Kyle Kozawalski, a sixth grader who had done most of his growing already. Ignored in his own class, Kyle was revered amongst the fifth graders, though he still took his cues from Philip. Bringing up the rear was Philip's younger brother Bryce, a pudgy third grader who only survived the Darwinian hazards of the bus stop because of his brother. There were no ready escape routes. Mendelssohn could feel tears pooling below his eyes. The pain registering throughout his body was like fire, and above it all was a piercing ring in his right ear.

"Well, what should we do?" Philip said.

"Philip, please." Mendelssohn could hear the whine in his voice, the tears that were barely being held back, and he knew the other boys could hear it, too.

"Please?" Philip said, laughing. Then the smile disappeared from his face, and in a disturbing tone he asked, "Please what?"

Mendelssohn's jaw was working, his mouth gesticulating rapidly, but nothing was coming out. He wanted to ask for mercy, but he knew those outside the herd were denied that luxury.

"Okay," Philip said, and began to move in.

Then, somewhere over the ringing and the fear consuming all of Mendelssohn's senses, he heard a new sound, one that made the other boys freeze.

"Wha... what was that?" Kyle said in his oafish, overgrown way, as if his tongue were too big for his mouth.

It came again—a shriek that washed over them like an icy wave, turning everything cold. Even Mendelssohn forgot his injuries and held his breath, trying to decide if the situation had actually managed to get worse. The boys looked up and down the street. They paced, weaving around within their group, the circle ever tightening. Soon they were standing back-to-back, defensive and ready, an eye searching in every direction.

Another scream.

They were about to run when Bryce extended a chubby arm and screamed, "Look!" The boys followed the invisible line that stretched from his finger to infinity and found something in a tree three driveways down. There was a pale, ghostly figure crouched in a lower branch. The light from a nearby lamppost didn't offer much in the way of detail, but it did hint at a reddish glow in the ghoul's eye.

"Whuh... whuh..." was all Philip Hampton could get out.

The figure sprung from the tree with a hideous shriek and seemed to almost fly: first to one tree, then another, then it was right on top of them.

"*It's a ghost!*" Bryce screamed.

The group exploded outward in five directions, seemingly propelled by their girlish screams. The phantom allowed them all to escape except Philip, who was clearly the dominant figure, making him the prime target. It swooped down screaming like a banshee and landed on Philip's back, knocking him to the ground and forcing the air out of him. Philip tried to crawl, but the creature was grabbing at his head and jumping up and down on his back as the bully began crying and blubbering, begging for help. The beast slapped the back of his head repeatedly, and though Philip wouldn't realize it until later that night, it also saturated him with urine. And it never stopped screaming throughout the entire attack. After a solid minute of torment that would require years of psychotherapy, Philip was allowed to break free. He ran home, never looking back or saying a word. All he could do was cry.

Alabaster walked over to Mendelssohn sporting a satisfied smile.

"Thanks, Alabaster."

The chimp wrapped his arms around Mendelssohn's waist and hooted softly into his stomach.

Mendelssohn kept Alabaster at his home overnight, and the chimp followed him to school the next day. Glimpses of him—sitting in a tree, swinging on the monkey bars, playing on the seesaw—were caught by several students, the most noteworthy reaction coming from Bryce Hampton, who fainted and fell face-first into his Salisbury steak. When the end of the day arrived, and Mendelssohn was looking forward to a leisurely stroll home in the afternoon sunshine, Mrs. Strebor reminded him about their meeting.

"I don't want you to worry, Mindy," she told him. "We'll find something you can do. By tomorrow you'll— *God in Heaven, what is that?!*"

Mendelssohn looked in the direction of Mrs. Strebor's horror and saw Alabaster, his face pressed against the window, his arms extended and palms lying flat to the glass. His fingers were tapping wildly.

"That's just Alabaster," he said. "It looks like he wants to play."

Mrs. Strebor had gone white. She whispered, "Play?"

"Yeah. Piano. He, uh... he plays... here, I'll show you."

Mendelssohn left the room and reappeared a few minutes later leading Alabaster by the hand. Mrs. Strebor let out a short, piercing yelp when they entered the room, and climbed atop her desk.

"It's okay," Mendelssohn said. "He's harmless."

Remembering Philip Hampton's experience of the previous night, however, he added, "For the most part."

In the corner of the classroom sat an aged upright piano beside a box filled with triangles and wood blocks and castanets and tambourines and finger cymbals. A colossal, colorful sign above the piano declared, *MUSIC BELONGS TO EVERYONE*, while a smaller sign below warned, *Handle instruments with care. They are not yours!*

Alabaster screeched eagerly and scurried to the piano, climbed the bench, and cracked his knuckles. He positioned his hands over the keyboard and drew in a long, deep breath through his flared nostrils. After a few seconds, he turned his head slowly and looked at Mendelssohn, who replied with a single nod.

It was Bach. *Toccata and Fugue in B Minor.* The first chords rattled the windows in the little classroom, sound exploding from the piano and raising dust from the long-forgotten music corner. As Alabaster played through the piece, Mendelssohn and his teacher watched intently, never exchanging a single word or look. Mendelssohn had heard it dozens of times, but it seemed more powerful with each playing—seemed to dig deeper into him, to places nothing else could venture. As for Mrs. Strebor, she was shocked to the point of stupidity.

When the piece was finished, Alabaster sat—his fingers trembling, the fur on the back of his neck standing at attention—fixed like a statue at the piano. Mendelssohn waited for the last echoing vibrations to die away, cast a sideways glance at his petrified teacher still perched on her desk, and began to clap. The applause signaled the end of the performance to Alabaster, and he leapt from the bench and ran and jumped throughout the room, shrieking happily and toppling chairs and desks in his wake.

Mrs. Strebor raised a hand to her breast and cried, "Oh, good Lord!" as she watched her most ordinary student chasing a prodigiously gifted albino chimpanzee pianist around her classroom at Openheyer Elementary School.

"He's really very nice," Mendelssohn called to her as he hurdled over books and papers and erasers and pencils and other educational debris Alabaster was strewing about the room. "He's just a little excited right now."

"Get him out of here!" Mrs. Strebor squealed. "Now, Mindy! Do you hear me? Right now!"

Mendelssohn stopped and turned to his teacher, his head shaking.

"I really hate it when you call me that."

"Get that animal out of here!" she screamed. "Both of you—get out of my classroom this instant! I *hate* monkeys! Do you hear? *I hate them!*"

Tears had begun to streak down her cheeks.

"Oh, God, just get it out of here, would you? Please take it away, please please please..."

Mendelssohn fought not to laugh at the simpering woman as she fell to her knees, shaking, huddled in the center of her desk. She glanced over, noticed the smile tugging at the corners of his mouth.

"Oh, you think this is funny?" she said.

"Well... yeah. A little. I mean, he's not going to hurt you."

"How do you know what he's going to do?"

"Because I know him. He loves me." Mendelssohn could feel himself standing a little taller, though he didn't know why. "He only plays for me, you know. No one else can get him to do it."

Mrs. Strebor climbed down from her desk. An instinct—an abstract force she neither knew nor understood—was pushing its way to the surface, pushing her to regain superiority, pushing her to cover her fear with the only feeling that could mask it: contempt.

A patronizing tone dripped from her voice when she said, "That's very nice, Mindy. A cute parlor trick."

"Parlor trick?"

"Yes," she said, smoothing her skirt out and erasing her tears.

Mendelssohn looked at Alabaster; the chimp simply smiled—his grin took up the bottom two-thirds of his head, and all of his teeth were visible. There was a moist sheen glistening off the pinks of his eyes.

"I guess maybe it is just a trick," Mendelssohn said, smiling at his friend. "But it's a trick he only does for me."

Mrs. Strebor didn't attempt to conceal her impatience.

"And?"

"Well, isn't that special somehow? Doesn't that mean something?"

"I can't imagine what that would mean."

"Don't some people have to be good at helping other people find what they're good at?"

His words sounded tangled. It was the innocent logic of children, and Mrs. Strebor could only blink at him.

Mendelssohn added, "Isn't that a teacher's gift?"

She coughed out a gravelly *harrumph* and said, "If I was gifted, I wouldn't be doing this."

"But you said everyone..." Mendelssohn started, and then sighed. As the breath blew out of him, he could feel something else on the tail of it, something escaping him that he might never get back. Mrs. Strebor was staring at him, and though she was the teacher, she was wearing the mask of a defiant child. He had tried to share something special with her—and it was only in this moment that he realized it wasn't Alabaster's talent, but his—and it was beyond her understanding. Not only did the truth escape her; he could see that she took a certain pride in her ignorance.

"I think I'll just go home," he mumbled, and turned to leave.

"Now, Mindy, I didn't mean to upset you," she said, though there was no apology in her tone. "There're just some things you're too young to understand."

Mendelssohn stopped, looked back at his teacher.

"I think you're the one who doesn't understand, Mrs. Strebor."

There was no judgment in his voice.

Every feature that could soften in her face—there weren't many—stiffened immediately, and a noticeable chill bit the air.

"I don't appreciate your tone, Mindy. This is very simple: If you had *taught* the monkey to play piano—that would be something. But just because he likes you enough to play for you—that doesn't mean anything. That's not a gift. Anyone can do that."

"Really?" Mendelssohn said. He led Alabaster back to the front of the classroom and offered Mrs. Strebor the chimp's hand. "Show me."

Album of the Year
Gavin Broom

January 1st, 2009 – At Austin's

The new year is in its infancy – minutes, maybe only seconds old – and born to a drunken world already neglecting it. The antique clock facing Austin's bar that had everyone spellbound now looks out at our backs and people who'd shaken hands and embraced are strangers once again.

In the photograph, Claire and I stand near the usual mob at the bar who do their best to spoil the shot. My hand sits on her waist. Her blonde head finds its nest on my shoulder and her smile is warm and crooked like she's stifling a laugh. James is in front of me, typically worse for wear, frozen in celebration, cheering with wide eyes and mouth. Next to him, in a white dress, Kerry blows the camera a kiss.

That night, the booze fuels talk of approaching thirtieth birthdays, promotions at work, subtle suggestions of overdue engagements that secretly terrify as much as the idea of weddings. There's talk of seizing the day, of the less worn path, of not settling like our parents, of making something of ourselves, of having big plans. The thing I notice, though, through all the hope and expectation captured on our faces, is that none of us know what's coming. We don't have a clue.

February 15th, 2009 – Birthday

It was James who suggested this inspired way to combine Valentine's Day and Claire's birthday while picking up some Best Boyfriend in the World points along the way. The result of this idea is a stereotypical Parisian taking a stereotypical photograph of two stereotypical tourists.

Claire and I are rosy-cheeked, wrapped in long coats and scarves at the top of the Eiffel Tower. It's impossible to tell if we're smiling or grimacing against the brutal chill. Over our shoulders, the crisp, grey city does its best to look as though it hasn't posed like this a million times already today. There's no such thing as privacy up here and other tourists sandwich us as they have their pictures taken or talk with their significant others and it makes me think of all the paths, all the billions of decisions that have been made independently across the globe to make us all share this moment. It makes me think of my own path.

Later that evening, back at the hotel, we sit at the bar and drink whisky until our blood thaws. The bartender is disinterested and surly until he realises we're Scottish and not English as he'd assumed. After that, he's our new best friend and the three of us drink and chat into the wee hours. When he announces that he's originally from Cameroon, bored with Paris and looking to move on, it ignites something in Claire. Excited, she grabs my hand and suggests we deliberately miss our return flight. Instead, she wants to withdraw her life savings and travel through Europe to the Far East, working on a farm in Switzerland, pouring drinks or waiting tables in Dubai, sleeping on a beach in Vietnam. Over and over, the bartender says what an excellent idea it is and the more he says it, the more animated Claire becomes and the more detached I find myself. She looks at me for a reaction and I smile but when I don't speak, she gives me back my hand

and leaves me with thoughts of paths and how unmade decisions are still decisions and unspoken words can still be heard.

April 1st, 2009 – April Fools

James' reason for surprising Kerry with a party and proposal on April Fools' Day is surprisingly simple and valid: she won't be expecting it. And he's right. When she walks into the function room, her hands shoot to her mouth, her knees buckle for a moment and she needs to be calmed by her sisters and friends. Eventually, she collects herself and even though she's crying, she's laughing when she says yes.

Claire asks me to take a photograph of Kerry's hand, now seemingly as complete as her life thanks to a chunk of compressed carbon set in a platinum band. I'm no expert on such things but I have to admit to being impressed by James' choice. It suits her hand; makes her fingers look slender and elegant. I can't help wondering how much it cost, how much James earns and, if it's more than me, what he did to deserve it. Any of it. I do as I'm told and take the photo. As I review the image, I notice the French tips on Kerry's fingernails and a patch of uneven fake tan around her wrist and my stomach flinches at what I suspect may be a ruse.

At ten o'clock, the DJ takes a break for the buffet and it's while we're eating that Claire raises a subject I knew was in the post from the moment James told me of his intentions. Still, I pretend to be taken aback and tell her I thought the plan was to go backpacking across Australia or cycle round the world or work on a salmon farm in Tibet or open an orphanage in Mozambique. That's when something changes, something leaves her eyes and whatever it is, wherever it goes, it doesn't come back.

June 21st, 2009 – Solstice

Every year, my dad made a big deal of the shortest night. For as long as I can remember, he talked about setting off in the car when the sun went down and driving until it rose the next morning, just to see where it would take him. Given that this allowed him about five or six hours driving time, I would tell him that he'd either end up just past Birmingham if he went south, somewhere in Caithness if he went north and in the sea if he went any other direction. Neither option sounded particularly appealing. He'd look annoyed when I said this. Apparently, I missed the point.

On this particular solstice evening, much like all the others, he's going nowhere. The doctor says he can't get home, the surgeon wants to talk to my mother in private about more procedures planned for the morning and the nurse gives him a hard, square cushion to hug on to when the coughing gets bad. The cushion has a face drawn on it in black marker; cock-eyed with its tongue sticking out of its grinning mouth. Dad thinks this is hilarious and while Mum's still away, he asks me to take a photo on my phone. He holds the pillow next to his face and strikes a matching pose. When I show him the result, he's delighted. Twins, he says. He asks if I can print a copy and bring it with me tomorrow. I tell him that if the surgeons have their way, he might not be in the best shape to look through photos. It'll be a piece of piss, he insists. A piece of piss.

On the drive home, Mum repeats her conversation with the surgeon and talks about how she feels things have run away in the last few weeks and everything's moving too fast. It's all I can do to keep driving because what I really want to do is pull over, take the phone out of my pocket, show her the photo and see if between us we can find anything that'll make us smile. The phone stays where it is, though, and the pack of glossy printer paper I buy after I drop Mum off isn't unwrapped until much, much later.

August 7th, 2009 – Satellites

Claire phoned me first. Being honest, it amazed me it wasn't the other way round and hadn't happened much earlier, especially as it had been a tough summer, during which I'd become well acquainted with the bottom of a bottle. Given these conditions, a drunken call in the middle of the night, begging for a reconciliation, wasn't so much likely as downright inevitable. I remember thinking it was good to be surprised. The feeling doesn't last.

We meet in a coffee shop in town the next evening and it's the first we've seen each other in three months. I have a latte. She orders a green tea of all things, which I read as a flag in the sand, a definite statement that things have changed and they're not changing back. For the next thirty minutes we're civil while we tiptoe through our conversational minefield and then she reaches into her bag – new, I notice – and hands me something I mistake for a birthday card. On the front of the card is a drawing of a teddy bear holding a balloon. Inside, there's a grainy, black and white photograph that looks like an image from a weather satellite. Just as I realise why a cloud looks like a tiny foot, it all falls into place and I become conscious that Claire's speaking to me, explaining something, saying my name, but the words are too bassy, too muffled, as though we're underwater. I don't move my head. I keep my eyes focused on that little foot. I let the waves of nausea crash and wash over me and wait for them to subside. Eventually, the tide goes back out.

It's only when she gets up that I notice the makings of a bump and puffiness in her cheeks. She tells me she'll be in touch and that I can be as involved as I want but, because we're still looking for different things, in every other regard it's business as usual. I'm left holding the photograph with the very tips of my fingers, as though it's made from the most delicate of porcelain. The sky is orange and shadows are long when I throw some money on the table. I notice that her cup of green tea hasn't been touched.

November 17th, 2009 – Removal

When I arrive at James' flat with the van, Kerry is somewhere else, just as she'd promised. I'm surprised at how little stuff he has and he tells me he travels light. I remind him that he's lived here for four years. He doesn't reply to that. Instead, he mutters about how he can't believe this is happening so close to Christmas and pays no attention when I say Christmas is really six weeks away and not that close at all. No sense in anyone doing stuff that makes them both unhappy, I say to him when it looks like he's pouting. No sense at all. He agrees.

In my haste to shift a chest of drawers, a photograph frame falls on the floor and cracks under my heel. The photo of Kerry and her dog is torn and just as I'm about to find James to apologise, I spot another picture underneath. This other, hidden photo is of the four of us at a restaurant table in Cyprus. James and I are in shirts and the women are in dresses; Claire blue and Kerry white. James is the only one without much of a tan because, I remember, he spent most of the holiday sitting in the shade at the pool bar drinking domestic lager and chatting up the Cypriot barmaid when he thought no one was looking. I try to recreate the emotions from that time, the things that were going through my head, the happiness I'm sure I must have felt. For a second, I almost have it – I'm nearly there – but then it all feels too far away and not just time-wise. I flatten the original photo back in the broken frame and although I'm not sure for whose benefit I'm doing it, I tear up the Cyprus photograph and put it in the bin.

His new place isn't as nice as he described it. It's dark, one bedroom and the smell of damp in the air pounces on me as soon as the door opens. James seems happy, though, so I try not to be too negative. We sit on cardboard boxes and share a four-pack as a reward for our efforts and he remarks about how strangely things have worked out, considering how they looked at the start of the year. I try to remember the thoughts about my path but the finer details escape me and the best I can do is explain that I'm convinced things were always going to work out this way, regardless of any plans. Except, I tell him, I thought he'd be the one to cheat on her. He laughs and for the second time today, he agrees.

December 31st, 2009 – At Austin's

The year has minutes – maybe seconds – left to live. Looking around, I see enough familiar faces to feel like this used to be home. Toasts are raised to what's left of 2009 and I'm reminded it's also the end of a decade, maybe even the end of an era, and this, along with turning thirty, makes me feel old; too old to stay here. Big Ben starts his preamble when I whisper in Kerry's ear that I want to leave. She smiles and without asking why, she follows me outside. I suspect she knows.

As far as I can recall, it's always windy at the bells. Tonight, though, it's calm and the cloudless, speckled night sky allows a frost to shroud us while we sit on the car park wall. Fireworks trace above as 2010 makes its entrance and I'm reminded of shooting stars and then of my dad. Through the explosions, I end up talking about him and I mention his unfulfilled plan for the summer solstice. She says I should do that. She says we should both do that and reckons it would be great if everyone did it. We could start a trend. She laughs at my raised eyebrow and insists it would be fun to see where we end up and what adventures might be waiting for us there. The way she explains it makes me understand what I think the whole world's been trying to tell me and I shiver, but not from the cold. A little later, we go back inside where once more the new year feels like it happened a long time ago. James and Claire are nursing soft drinks in separate corners of the bar with their halves of the usual mob. They glower while conversations happen around them. I'm not sure of the meaning of the smile I send to Claire. Maybe I'm apologising. Maybe I'm saying that none of us know what the next twelve months will bring. Either way, she manages to send a smile back. I haven't brought my camera with me tonight, so none of this is documented and if in years to come my kid decides that he or she needs to know what Daddy got up to on this particular Hogmanay, they're just going to have to take my word for it.

Out of Steam Punk and Zombies Comes Bruce Lee

Jenny Ortiz

Use only that which works and take it from any place you can find it. – Bruce Lee

Strewn on the couch are second hand clothes and old kung fu movies. East likes Bruce Lee the best; she knows everyone says it, but Bruce Lee was a badass motherfucker; his son, too. They were real cool. With an untoasted Pop-tart, East sits on top of the clothes and watches *Enter the Dragon*, alone.

Later on, when the movie is finished, East goes into the kitchen for some cereal. She opens the fridge only to find the milk carton empty. Throwing on her leather jacket, she waves to her fish and heads to the supermarket. This is the only thing she hates about the real world. The things she needs don't appear in front of her, she has to go out and get them.

As East walks down the block, she once again concludes that as much as she misses certain things that made her life easy, she would not be some kind of sleeper cell; that's what she'd promised herself when she left the world created by the Authors and entered the real world. She forgot about the steam punk nation she'd been born into and settled in New York. She'd been a nomad there and had nothing and no one to miss. Sometimes East thought about Roan, the way they'd travelled through forests and swamps on their way to... where?

She couldn't remember what ending the Authors had planned. A face off with her brother, Ian. No, she shakes her head as she walks down the block to the corner, where the red awning of the supermarket is drooping low and is threatening to fall on the crates of dry apples and thick skinned oranges. She isn't going to spend her youth waiting for the Authors to pick up where they left off. Let Ian control that world, overthrow the king or the corporation; she isn't even sure who is in power anymore. Her leader now is the President of the United States. Though she isn't sure what democracy means, East believes it's better than an army of zombies that keeps the population in check.

The only thing East really misses about her old life is the show Dinopups. She is wearing a shirt, with a Dinopups character on it. It reminds her of the card game that went with the show and how she'd played with Ian. She never lost. She doesn't have the cards or the show or, for that matter, anyone to play with anymore.

East doesn't like to think about the past. Her story had once been written with enthusiasm, only to be left midway through. She and the other characters were in a perpetual wait, repeating the same actions, walking in circles, pretending to be lost. Having clawed her way out of the swamp, East had pulled herself out from between the green ink and white lined paper. Pushed the words off her skin and took a job at a Laundromat. East avoided other characters, the ones who escaped and certainly the ones still in stories. In every book, she could hear them calling for her to come back.

But as she makes her way to the open fridge in the back of the supermarket, East thinks about all of the people she left behind. She knows the only reason she's thinking about the story and the past is because of The Grappler, Jude here. He'd moved from her story to another collapsed story, only to be abandoned. He'd always been a good character—she liked his smile and the way his boots were always covered with desert sand. But the Authors took him out of her story because she was supposed to only have interest in Roan. But Roan isn't around anymore and the other day, Jude and East went out on their third official date. He's coming over later tonight for a movie, some snacks, and wine. Along with the milk, East buys a pack of condoms.

***

He's late. Two whole Bruce Lee movies late. East watches the popcorn bag turn in the microwave, while the credits run on the television. After taking a large swallow of chocolate milk, East moves toward her fish tank. The red and orange fish glide around unaware of her presence. They make large circles in the tank, ignoring the plastic submarine and the clay mermaids sitting on the rocks. She imagines that being a character is very much like being a fish. She was given food, and a daily schedule. Her friends and her family were already waiting for her. For a moment, she wishes she still had the security of knowing Roan loved her. She wonders, if it had been written that they'd love each other right away, why she left him behind.

The fish don't jump like East does to the sound of knocking on her door. The popping sound follows her as she opens the door. Wet and panting Jude stands in front of her with a big smile. He's wearing his tattered black coat and dusty boots.

"They're writing the ending of our story."

"What are you talking about?"

"I woke up this morning and was in the forest, looking for you and Roan."

"Looking?"

"I work for the cooperation, duh. I've been trailing the two of you. Of course I'm only working for them to get revenge for my wife's death… but that doesn't matter, what matters is that I was trailing you in the story."

"You just woke up in the story? How's that possible?"

"We are characters."

"I haven't been pulled back into the story."

"Not yet, but I think you'll be written in sometime tomorrow."

"But I work tomorrow. And I'm pulling a double shift because the rent is due at the end of the week."

"What's that matter? We're going back home."

She looks around at the things she's bought and rearranged so carefully. The couch from IKEA she'd assembled on her own, photos of the day she adopted her fish, the magazine subscriptions, the television, Bruce Lee.

"I think I need a drink," she says.

***

They sit together in a booth at the Left of Center, a bar that caters specifically to characters. East pulls her sleeves over her hands as the waitress, a woman styled like a 1950s pin-up, brings them their beers. The bar is crowded. Mondays are always crowded. Authors reread their weekend dribble and cut whole passages, full of characters. Little than half of those characters filter into the real world, looking for something to do. East hates being around them, but Jude takes her anyway. A stock character tries to buy East a drink, which amuses Jude. She slumps into the booth and stares straight ahead, pretending to be brain dead. After a few minutes, the stock character shrugs at Jude, and finds himself a flat character to dance with. Full characters only come to the bar because it's the best discarded description of one. Cheap drink and good music could cover up the crowds. Ladyhawke's Professional Suicide is playing and Jude asks her if she wants to dance; she's about to say yes, but a gang of stereotypes walk in and take over the dance floor. The music becomes frantic and the air dense.

It's at these times when she remembers her past with sadness: the smell of the trees and the soft, mud like texture of the ground under her bare feet. Towards the end of her time in that world, she stopped using shoes. Gave up the worn down ankle boots for a thin layer of dirt on her skin. Had Roan disapproved? She couldn't remember.

"Can we go?" she says, looking at Jude.

"We just got here."

"I hate this fucking place."

"You wanted to get a drink."

"Why couldn't we go to a normal bar?"

"Because this is where our people are."

"They're not my people."

"And humans are? You can't do anything with them."

"I'm leaving."

"And going where? You going to go see another Bruce Lee movie? That's really assimilating to the real world."

She ignores him and zippers up her jacket against the wind. Jude's right. She's lonely here. No, not lonely, haunted by nothing. East realizes now that nothing has a weight. It isn't heavy, but uncomfortable, making itself known. Whenever a Bruce Lee film ends and the credits are flashing on the screen, East feels the nothing. She doesn't feel it when she's with Jude, but she hates his reasoning as to why: they'll only be fulfilled if they're reconnected to the story. She crosses the street, narrowly avoiding a speeding car. She doubts the driver sees her; she's like a sliver of black paper floating in the dark.

A guy in a biker jacket opens the door to another bar, a bar with real people inside. She mumbles thanks and slips in, avoiding the guy in the front checking ID. Though no one is smoking, there is the smell of cigarettes on everyone's clothes and the sound of the cash register is shrill and overpowers the sound of people talking. East slips through the crowd and takes a seat at the end of the bar, orders a beer, and begins to watch the people. She likes how the girls' sleek metallic colored skirts crawl up their thighs as they dance in place. The music is bad, but no one seems to notice.

When she notices him, he is standing with a girl in crème colored pants too tight for her thighs, but she's still attractive. He's standing next to her talking, his face close to hers, and he is bent slightly to meet her. When he stands up straight, he's tall, thin, and with his white buttoned down looks more like a sheet of paper than East does.

A heat settles in East's thighs and right below her breasts as she watches the girl shrug and move away from the paper-like man. He sighs and puts his beer bottle on a table nearby and leaves. East follows him all the way down to the subway. She luckily has a MetroCard and quickly follows him towards the platform where he waits for the A. It's already one in the morning, and from the looks of another man on the platform, they just missed one. They'll have to wait another thirty minutes. Putting on her headphones, East chooses an instrumental to play while watching the paper man.

East likes taking the train; she likes watching the people. They slowly become her characters, each one with a story she won't abandon. Sometimes, she'll feel the urge to write one down on paper, but she never does.

He doesn't notice her until they're on the train and she's standing next to him, her eyes on an ad by his head. She smiles at him.

"You were at the bar with your girlfriend."

"No, she's a friend."

"But you want her to be your girlfriend?"

"I—I don't know… Do I know you?"

"No." She pauses. "I'm East."

"Nice to meet you," he says, not looking at her. She is still smiling.

***

He has travel magazines on his coffee table. East picks one up and begins reading about the fantastic beaches of Malaysia. She knew a boy from Malaysia, tall and athletic. He didn't talk much, but told funny jokes. She can't remember any of them now. He only worked at the Laundromat for a few weeks before he started school. Once he started, he never came back. They had washers and dryers on campus. Now the only people working aside from herself were the manager, Kim, and Paul; none of them liked to talk much.

"I get them for free from the adjunct faculty lounge. The *Popular Mechanics*, too."

"Are you a teacher?"

"Not yet. I'm a graduate student. I get a stipend for helping a few of the professors with their classes."

"That sounds interesting."

"Yeah, it is. What do you do?"

"I work in fashion. I'm responsible for organizing and separating different colors and textures of the clothes to be used on the models. "

"Sounds pretty important."

"It is. One slip up and a whole week's worth of fashion statements are destroyed."

"Are you thirsty?"

"No."

He's already in the kitchen and doesn't hear her. The furniture in his apartment is sparse, except for the old couch and the stack of books neatly against the off white wall where the television should be. On the bottom of the stack is a biography on Bruce Lee. Carefully, East pulls the book from the bottom without toppling the other books on the modern world and literary theory. She flips through the pages until she finds the photos and examines each one.

"Are you into him?" he asks.

"Yeah. I have all his movies. I've read this. Did you know he pitched the show Kung Fu? In the end, they didn't cast him. But he said the moves in the show were more ballet than—"

"I don't know much about him. My friend was studying alternative philosophy and left this behind," he says curtly, avoiding her eyes.

He hands her a beer and they move to the couch. They look at the bare wall silently. Their arms are touching and she can feel the tension in his body. There's nothing to keep her eyes focused on and the beer in her hand is warm. She sets it down by her feet and puts her head on his shoulder. Looking at his forearm, East examines the black hairs sticking up and the veins bulging slightly. He's breathing evenly, which surprises her. She wants to ask him about the girl with the crème colored pants, but doesn't. Where the walls meet, there is an opening to her story. She knows he can't see it; the branches of the trees are sticking out and leaves are slowly crawling on the wall. The shadow of a man passes through the trees. She shudders; he puts his arm around her.

"Do you have a bedroom?"

"Yeah," he says.

She follows him and before they even get inside, she begins to remove her clothes. The floor under her feet is muddy and in the distance she can hear Roan's voice. He's looking for her. East closes her eyes and lets the stranger kiss her. Sex with him is like a warm finger flipping through the pages of a book. She ignores him as he whispers the name Abigail and focuses on her movements. When they're finished, she gets dressed and leaves without saying goodbye. She takes with her the newest copy of *Popular Mechanics* for the ride home. She isn't particularly interested in Abigail's Bruce Lee.

On the train ride home, she reads the articles as a way to avoid making eye contact with the zombies sitting around her. Even holding her breath, East can't escape the smell of iron and feces coming off their dirty, broken bodies. They aren't very bright, so she can get off at her stop without worrying about them following her. As she makes her way out, a man and his girlfriend walk in. East doesn't pause to check on them; instead she makes her way home.

On her way up the stairs to her apartment she finds Jude leaning against her door. She smiles at him.

"Where did you go?"

"I went home with someone."

"Because of the story? You have no choice. You're going to wake up one morning and find yourself back there. What are you going to do, crawl back to the real world every night?"

"If I tell you I'm good, you will think I am boasting. But if I tell you I'm no good, you know I'm lying," she mumbles slowly as she opens the door.

"What?"

Jude is standing in the doorway.

"It's only the best line Bruce Lee ever said." She pauses, her body is slumped slightly. "I think that it reflects this situation quite well. I'm going to do whatever I need to so that I can stay here. If I have to cut off zombie heads in the subway or get pregnant—"

"Is that why you slept with that guy? To get pregnant?"

"How did you know I slept with him?"

"You slept with him? I was just taking a guess. East… It's not normal for us to be with them like that."

"If I tell you I'm good—"

"Stop saying that."

"Okay, how about this one: Love is like a friendship caught on fire. In the beginning a flame, very pretty, often hot and fierce, but still only light and flickering—"

"East, stop," he says as he pulls her towards him.

"As love grows older, our hearts mature and our love becomes as coals, deep-burning and unquenchable," she says smiling. "Pretty, huh?"

"East."

"If you always put limits on everything you do, physical or anything else, it'll spread into your work and into your life. There are no limits. There are only plateaus, and you must not stay there, you must go beyond them… He said that too."

East pushes away from Jude.

"Why are you saying all this?"

"Why am I? How am I capable of memorizing every one of Bruce Lee's famous quotes? Why can I work in a Laundromat or have a one night stand with a stranger? Why would the Authors build all of this in my character if I was supposed to do what they want me to do in a faraway place that doesn't mean anything to me?"

"You're the main character."

"Do I have to be? Why can't they make another character? We've evolved. We're no longer the characters we were."

"That's not true."

"You haven't killed anyone while we've been here. You haven't talked about revenge or even thought about your dead wife. No, every night you come over and we eat Chinese food and listen to music. You're more out of character than I am." She pauses. "Bruce Lee says—"

"Please tell me. Tell me what Bruce Lee says. He's dead, East. And you know what he did when he was alive? He made movies. He became a character. He wanted to be one of us. So shut up and come back to the story." His shoulders are slumped. "We can be immortal."

"The key to immortality is first living a life worth remembering," she recites another quote; this time she says it as she walks towards the kitchen table. She sits down and looks at him. "As you think, so shall you become... that's what he says... said. I think it's appropriate for us... don't you think?"

"You're selfish. What about Roan? You're going to leave him alone?"

"If the Authors let you remember me, remember the time we visited the Empire State building."

"Night, East."

"Night, Ju— Grappler."

After watching him leave, East turns off the lights and turns on the television, but doesn't focus on it. Instead she drinks some milk from the carton, and sits on the couch, waiting to fall asleep. She thinks about the things she needs to do for work and wonders when she should buy a pregnancy test. She avoids the sounds of the jungle coming from her bathroom, closing her ears off to Roan's crackling fire or to Jude's boots crunching the plants on the ground, as he prepares to kill.

Three Dates in Orlando
Daniel McDermott

Bluette

It was the vomit that ended things. I'm pretty sure. Vomit does that to people: scares them away, makes them cringe, makes them question their most recent decisions. And Bluette's vomit was no ordinary, run-of-the-mill, I-have-the-flu-will-someone-please-hold-my-hair-back kind of vomit, nor was her regurgitation a single occurrence. No. Bluette's vomit was the projectile kind, with a far-spewing arch normally reserved for garden hoses, rainbows, and powder-chucking snow blowers. And her nauseating episode was threefold: once in the bar on an open-toed pack of screeching coeds, once on the rust-colored cobblestone of Church Street before a cheering crowd of beer-handed onlookers, and once in the parking lot, in the car, in the driver's seat, on my lap.

I had a hunch about that third time.

"Should I wait a little bit?" I asked, the ignition key inserted but the car not yet started. "Do you feel like you're gonna be sick again?"

Bluette slumped her petite, 100-pound frame into the front passenger seat, her frilly yellow skirt pushed up inappropriately high, an errant bite of dirty-blond hair tucked in the left corner of her mouth, and a heaving cadence to her sour breath. She turned to me, sat upright, and leaned in across the cup holders and change console with eyes wide and mouth open, as if to say, "Yes. Thank you for asking. I do have to vomit again. Look!"

It was our second date. It was our last date. I sped down I-4, pushing the limits of my dilapidated, 4-cylinder Honda with viscous stomach bile seeping into my crotch. The scent was worse than foul-smelling things are supposed to smell, like putrid, horrifying, defecated things not of this world, like a weapons-grade version of that ubiquitous hotdog odor that lingers around deli counters and fast-food joints. It lives in my brain, this smell, tattooed into my memory. It waits for morning breakfasts and Thanksgiving dinners. It comes alive and swims to the front of my temporal lobe to say hello.

"Forget about your mother's candied ham," It says. "Put down that crispy bacon. Throw away that cheeseburger and remember, forever, the little French woman who threw-up in your lap."

Nancy

I thought the idea of a gym date was cool: music, raging endorphins, a pumped physique, and the knowledge that your partner is at least mildly self-respecting (if not a bit narcissistic). But I didn't realize that Nancy's daughter would be coming to the gym with us – I didn't realize Nancy had a daughter at all – and I didn't realize her daughter's biological father was a personal trainer at the gym, and I didn't realize her daughter was still an infant, and I didn't realize that Nancy would be breastfeeding her infant daughter on our date, in the gym, on the exercise bike.

It's not often that you are spectator to the suckling of your date's nipple. And, if you are, it's usually not on the first date, and it's usually not in public, and it's certainly not nourishingly so.

For some reason, I did not feel inspired to exercise while the baby fed and the breast explored the exterior of its stretchy red sports bra, despite Nancy's pleasant assurance.

"You can go ahead and start without us. She'll be done in a minute," she said, peddling away, stroking the little bald head of her nipple-sucking child. But I decided, instead, to awkwardly converse with Nancy's vascular, neck-less, cologne-and-gel-scented ex-husband.

"How's it going there, buddy?" said the ex, with a vice-grip handshake and an arm-swinging shoulder slap. He seemed fine with the scenario – with me, and his ex-wife, and his daughter, and his ex-wife's milk-spigot-breast – which didn't seem normal given that, considering the baby's fledgling age, he couldn't be more than a year or so removed from the making of this adorable, publically breast-chomping little girl.

"How's it going?" I said to the meaty ex. "Say, could you tell me where the restroom is?"

"Right through those doors," he pointed, with a calloused, karate-chop hand.

"Thanks. I'll be right back."

The gym was relatively empty, just a gum-chewing high school kid manning the front desk and a couple spandex-clad women trolling through a rack of dumbbells. The quickening swish of my nylon track pants carried me away from Nancy, her ex, their child, and her exposed bosom. And, fortunately for me, the restroom was located near the front exit, and the front exit emptied into the parking lot, and in the parking lot I could see my vomit-scented Honda, and I drove my Honda back out onto International Drive, down Westwood Boulevard, and back to my single bedroom apartment and my single life.

Laura

She said it over pizza; that's what's really disturbing. It wasn't late at night, we weren't playing Truth or Dare, and we weren't clinking shot glasses or licking salt from our wrists. It would have been weird regardless, but it's just not the kind of thing I wished to associate with pizza. Before Laura, pizza was birthday parties, college late-nights, and little league victories. But now pizza is simply Laura, our third date, and her twisted past.

She was talking about her father, how he is tall, handsome, impressively athletic, a financial executive for a large credit card company who now spends most of his time in South America, and that she sort of had a relationship with him a few years ago.

"What do you mean... a *relationship*?" I asked.

"You know, like an actual relationship," she said, her mouth half full of pepperoni and dough, "like a boyfriend/girlfriend kind of relationship... a sexual thing. But it's OK; he's not my real dad; I was adopted."

My heart began to palpitate. The pizza tasted bitter and oniony, the cheese now infused with Laura's rancid dysfunction.

"How old were you when you were adopted?" I asked.

"Just a baby... why?"

"What about your mother?"

"Oh, she doesn't know. She'd kill me if she ever found out."

"I see."

"Oh no!" she raised a French-tipped hand to her mouth, still chewing. "Does it bother you?"

Yep.

"I mean, it's over now. I promise. It was just for like a year or so in my early twenties."

"And how old are you now?" I asked, still palpitating, wanting to scream and cry and run and phone the authorities.

"Twenty-five."

"And even though you've, uh, *been* with him you still call him *dad*?"

"Well, not really. I mean, he'll always be my daddy–"

Gross.

"–but now I mostly call him Roy."

"I see… Roy… right."

Laura narrowed her eyes, scrunched them between brow and cheek, tossed a nibbled chard of crust onto a plate-side stack of red and green napkins, and reclined into our wooden booth with arms folded.

"It's not like he forced me or anything."

I didn't know what to say. People who have had sexual relationships with their parents should not be talking to me, or dating me, or casually eating pizza. People who have had sexual relationships with their parents should be in large gated buildings with white-collared doctors and stockpiled Lithium supplies. They should be heroin addicts, carnies, or homeless street-folk who dance on park benches and whisper to statues. And their parents should be locked up, or caned, or burned at the stake. And, yes, the same goes for someone who adopts a child and waits for her to grow up before perpetrating his sexual deviance. Moreover, a minimum $100,000 fine should be imposed on any man whose daughter refers to him as "Roy".

I did not lecture or ridicule Laura; I pitied her. But I was not prepared to deal with her borderline reality. So I paid the bill, said goodbye to Laura, said goodbye to pizza, stepped from the crisply air-conditioned eatery into the torrid Orlando humidity, revved up the vomit-smelling, nipple-escaping, Roy-evading Honda, broke my apartment lease with eight months remaining, and drove back to New Jersey.

The Werebear Who Wished to Come in from the Rain

Mike Sweeney

There are innumerable jokes to be made about the Garden State in some quarters, but if you've ever seen Central Jersey in late July, just after the azaleas have bloomed and just before the cicadas come out to sing in August, you'd have no problem believing why the nation's third state was nicknamed so. Read the letters of the Revolutionary War soldiers – Colonial, British, and Hessian alike – for their description of what New Jersey once was before industry and chemical. An earthly paradise where anything would grow, it was said.

And, today, in Central Jersey – the part that identifies with neither Philadelphia nor New York – that's still true. The land is rich and green like in the days of old.

Well, it is in spots, anyway.

There is no better time to observe the lush greenery of Jersey vegetation than during a summer rainstorm, the kind that move in from the south and berate the coastal counties before sweeping off into the Atlantic just as quickly as they appeared. The water soaks the carpet of green grass that covers the rich horse farms and the small suburban homes alike. The rain renews the ubiquitous red oaks, the stately yew trees, and the solemn weeping willows, replacing what the day's heat has wilted away.

It's a moment of reverence.

Time seems to slip away and the land is what it always has been. Things that once were are again, things old and unseen. They roam the earth they called their own long before there was a New Jersey or even an America. They wander here and there and, occasionally, when the ashen sky cracks and opens, they ask to come in from the rain.

***

Little Ashley May Rue was by all accounts a well-mannered and polite little girl. Quiet, but strong, it was said. She was her mother's rock in the days and weeks after her father's death. Her teachers all thought she would do well and the neighbors all thought she would keep her mom – and her little baby brother – anchored and sane in the difficult years that lay ahead.

It was a lot to ask of an eight-year-old, but Ashley May never complained or cried. It was like she knew something the others didn't.

But even if she hardly ever showed it, she missed playing whiffle ball with her Daddy and her cousins in the backyard, where the above ground pool was a home run and the swing set was a foul. She missed her Daddy holding the back of her bike – the pink sparkly one with the Power Puff Girls seat – as she wobbled and wavered along the sidewalk before lunch. Mostly, she missed the trips down the shore and the long walks with her Daddy in the sun, while Mommy sat feeding little Ben his bottle.

When she felt sad about not being able to do those things with her Daddy anymore, or when she just felt sad about all the things that had happened, the one thing that could always make her feel better was the rain.

It was her Mommy's own daddy who taught her to sit with the garage open on the late summer afternoons when the thunderstorms would roll in from the south and drench the world for one half hour or maybe two.

Grandpa showed Ashley May just the right distance – the length of an old picnic-table bench – to sit from the end of the garage so that you could feel the rain passing by without ever getting wet. They'd sit side-by-side in the rusty old beach chairs, the webbing frayed and yellow, and hum a song as they watched the water fall in sheets. Or sometimes, they would say nothing at all, and Grandpa and Ashley May would just hold hands and let their arms swing lightly as they stared off into the deluge.

It was where Ashley May learned to think of nothing when she wanted to think of everything. It was where she learned to find the calm even when everything around her made her want to cry.

Of course, her Grandpa was dead now too. From the cigarettes he smoked, they told her.

But Ashley May still loved looking at the rain.

It was three o'clock and almost as if on schedule, the slate sky began to crack and patter and another afternoon thunderstorm commenced. Little Ben was upstairs sleeping and Ashley May would have at least an hour to herself before she needed to change and feed him. She hoped the rain would last the whole hour.

She stopped using the beach chairs to watch the rain, as it didn't seem right to sit in them without Grandpa. So she stood – and occasionally twirled a little like a ballerina – exactly one picnic-table-bench-length from the edge of the garage and let her eyes and mind drift off into the sheets of rain and the occasional streak of lighting.

***

In truth, Ashley May wasn't quite thinking of nothing as the Werebear approached. She was concentrating on the poplar tree that dominated the front lawn of her family's house. She was earnestly trying to decide if it was called "poplar" because it was a popular type of tree. At least two of their neighbors had one as well, so it didn't seem that strange of an idea. She was just deciding her theory might have merit when the Werebear's nose poked around the corner of the open garage.

Ashley May had seen a great many animals – deer, wild turkeys, raccoon, and, of course, bunny rabbits – while watching the rain. But this was her first bear. The turkeys – loud and brazen – had given her quite a start. The bear didn't alarm her quite as much, as he was quiet. But he also was quite big and uncomfortably close. She took three steps back and looked to the door that led into the house at the back of the garage.

The Werebear cleared his throat and spoke. "Please don't be frightened, young miss."

Most people would be more than scared not just by a bear, but by one that spoke. But Ashley May had seen a great many things in her eight years and she wasn't frightened. Not quite, anyway.

"You can talk?" she said. It seemed a good idea to her to get that out in the open straight away.

"Yes," said the Werebear, in a deep, smoky baritone. "I can also catch cold." He let his eyes drift up to the rain pouring down on his snout and shook himself a bit to show that his fur was getting quite inundated.

Little Ashley May Rue furrowed her brow. This was a pickle. Her mother had been quite clear on what she was supposed to say to any visitors while she was away at work. Ashley May had repeated her mom's words exactly – to the social worker, to the mailman, to the college student who tried to sell her cable TV. But she didn't know what she was supposed to say to a bear, let alone a talking bear.

The Werebear cleared his throat again. "I don't mean to be forward, young miss, but might I – just for a few moments – come in from the rain?"

"You won't eat me?" said Ashley May, asking what seemed to her an honest, if slightly rude, question.

The Werebear's snout twisted into a frown. He exhaled disgustedly and turned to head down the driveway.

"Wait!" Little Ashley May Rue cried. "You…you can come in."

"Are you sure?" said the Werebear in his rich rumble of a voice.

"Yes," said Ashley May. "For a little while, anyway."

The Werebear nodded and lumbered into the garage, blocking out Ashley's May's view of the rain – of everything – before sitting on her right.

Ashley May didn't like this. It was where her Grandpa used to sit. She wasn't sure she had done the right thing.

"Grizzly," said the Werebear.

"What?"

"You were wondering what type of bear I am."

Ashley hadn't been but she didn't say so. Instead, she asked, "Do all grizzly bears talk?"

"No," laughed the Werebear. "I'm special. And I'm not entirely a bear."

"Not entirely?" asked Little Ashley May Rue.

"I used to be a person. A long, long time ago. Or at least I think I was. That's how I learned to talk."

"But now you're a bear?"

"A werebear is the precise term. You see, something happened. I used to be a human, then I was a bear and a human. After a while, I just stayed a bear."

"Do you like it?"

"It's all I know now," said the Werebear. "It's been so long since I was a person."

"What's the best part?"

"Eating little girls," said the Werebear. Then he turned his head to look at Ashley May and laughed a loud and hearty laugh. He sat back on his hind legs and rubbed his belly with his front paws as he guffawed to show the little girl what a good joke he'd made. Ashley May laughed with him though she didn't quite know why.

The Werebear shifted back onto all fours and walked around the garage a bit. He sniffed at the old rusty snow shovels, pawed a bit at the stacks of bound newspapers, and cast a disparaging eye at old the picnic-table bench Ashley May used to mark the correct distance for watching the rain.

"Where is your mommy?" he asked after a fashion.

"At work, but she'll be home in a few minutes," Little Ashley May Rue replied dutifully, saying exactly what her mother had told her to say.

"And your daddy?"

Ashley May was quiet for a full minute before answering. She waited until the Werebear moved back to her side before speaking.

"My Daddy's dead," she finally said.

"I see," said the Werebear. "Well, I am sorry to hear that. It must be hard on you being here all alone."

Ashley May didn't say anything more. She stared off into the rain. She remembered that the rain made things better, made her feel safe. She wanted to be safe. She wanted the Werebear to leave, didn't want to hear his breathing through his thick fangs, didn't want to listen to the way he subtly sniffed at her. She liked the silence with her Grandpa, but with the Werebear it just made her more uneasy. Ashley May desperately searched for something to say. She blurted out the first thing that came into her mind.

"Do you know Winnie the Pooh?" she said somewhat sheepishly.

"You know, I could eat you all in maybe three gulps," said the Werebear

"What?"

The Werebear stopped looking at the rain. He moved his bulk full round Ashley May, blocking out her view again. When he spoke, his voice was still deep, but had an edge to it.

"I said, 'I could eat you all in maybe three gulps.' Shall we find out?"

"You said you wouldn't eat me!" cried Little Ashley May Rue.

The Werebear laughed and it was not a nice laugh.

"I said no such thing. I never answered you. I was walking away when you stopped me. When you invited me in from the rain."

Ashley May took two quick steps backwards and the Werebear lunged forward positioning his snout an inch away from her nose. "Going somewhere, young miss?"

Ashley May tried not to cry. She said the only thing she could think of to save herself.

"Do you like babies?"

"What?!" growled the Werebear.

"Do you like babies?" repeated Little Ashley May Rue.

The Werebear nodded slowly. "Of course. Babies taste best. So soft and tender. One big bite." He clamped down his jaws to show Ashley May just how he would eat one.

"My brother... my baby brother. He's upstairs."

"Mmmm-hmmm," said the Werebear. He turned his nose to the air and sniffed hard twice. "Yes, yes he is."

"You could take him – instead of me."

"I could," said the Werebear.

"He tastes better than me." Ashley May's voice was small and cold.

"Why shouldn't I take you both?" asked the Werebear.

"Because I have the key to the door to the house," said Little Ashley May Rue. "It's metal and you can't break it down."

"Can't I?" scoffed the Werebear.

"No, you can't," said Ashley May. "At least not without making a lot of noise and attracting attention."

The Werebear nodded. "All right. You open the door for me. And I won't eat you. But I want to hear you say it again."

"Say what?"

"Say, you want me to eat your little baby brother and not you. Say it for me again."

His snout was right next to her cheek and Ashley May could feel the Werebear's breath, wet and foul.

"You promise you won't eat me? For real this time?" Ashley May said.

"I promise," said the Werebear. "For real, I promise."

"My brother," Ashley May whimpered. "I choose my baby brother. Eat him."

The Werebear laughed his dark, edgy laugh again. He didn't rub his belly. "Now that wasn't so hard, was it?"

Little Ashley May Rue reached into the pocket of her shorts – the denim ones with the SpongeBob face on both back pockets – and pulled out a small key. Her breathing was shallow and fast and she tried to slow it. She stepped to the door, placed the key in the lock and turned it. She felt an almost instant relief.

"There," she said, stepping aside.

The Werebear brushed passed her and placed his paws on the door. A smile, if you could call it that, played on his snout. The Werebear didn't normally go out of his way to be cruel, but he didn't like this little girl very much. He couldn't quite help himself.

"You know," he said in his thick, smoky voice, "it's really too bad your Daddy's gone and left you here all alone."

Ashley May swallowed hard and said what she said to all the others – to the mailman, to the social worker, to the man selling cable TV.

"I said my Daddy was dead. I didn't say he was gone."

She heard the door to the house open and covered her ears as the Werebear growled in agony, his roar echoing like thunder in the garage before trailing off into whimpers and the limp scratching of claws on concrete as he was pulled into the house.

Little Ashley May Rue still very much loved her Daddy, but she hated to watch him feed.

She turned her back and forced herself to focus on the downpour, the way her Grandpa taught her, and thought of nothing till everything just drifted away.

BRUCE J. BERGER is a graduate of the University of Connecticut and Harvard Law School and a former Executive Editor of the Harvard Law Review. He is a senior partner at the Washington, DC law firm Hollingsworth LLP. When not practicing law, he plays senior baseball and writes fiction, participating in a workshop at the Writers' Center in Bethesda, MD. The story "Nate and Adel" is the first in a collection of sixteen linked stories he completed earlier this year. He lives in Silver Spring, Maryland, with his wife, Laurie, an equestrian, and two dogs.

Z. Z. BOONE'S fiction has been nominated for the Pushcart Prize, The Best of the Web, and storySouth's Million Writers Award. Work has appeared in *Smokelong Quarterly, Annalemma, The MacGuffin, Third Wednesday, Swill, FRiGG, Wigleaf, decomP, Word Riot, Pank, Monkeybicycle,* and other terrific places.

GAVIN BROOM lives in the Scottish countryside with his wife and his cat. He's had work published in *Menda City Review, Bound Off, Espresso Fiction, flashquake* and *SFX* amongst others. At time of writing, he doesn't own a house at the beach.

KEVIN BROWN has had work published in over seventy journals and was nominated for a 2007 Journey Award and a Pushcart Prize. His first book, *Ink On Wood*, is scheduled to be published in the summer of 2010.

KATE DELANY'S previous publications include a book of poetry, *Reading Darwin*, published by Poets Corner Press. Her fiction and poetry has appeared in such magazines and journals as *Art Times, Barrelhouse, Chicken Piñata, Jabberwock Review, Philadelphia Stories* and *Spire Press*. She teaches in the English department at Rowan University in Glassboro, NJ.

ANDREW FRANKEL is a young and virile writer born and raised among the mysterious pines of Southern New Jersey. It is there that he currently makes his home. As always, he is ecstatic to have his terrible gibberish bound and printed at someone else's expense.

EIRIK GUMENY is a person, a consumer of both oxygen and coffee, taking up space in various parts of New Jersey. He is the editor of *Jersey Devil Press*, author of the novel *Exponential Apocalypse*, and folder of origami cranes. He is thrilled to have included himself in this anthology, but is more thrilled to be done editing the damn thing.

M. R. LANG is watching you read this and doesn't like your haircut. Each of his stories has a secret slight against you, but it's nothing personal.

DANIEL MCDERMOTT is a writer and founding editor of *Bananafish Magazine*. His work has appeared recently in *Fray Quarterly, Monkeybicycle, Writers' Bloc, The Murky Fringe*, and other publications. After many years of speech therapy, hypnotherapy, acupuncture, and an unfortunate incident with a Shaman (for which his court appearance is still pending), Daniel can finally pronounce the word "hippopotamus." Find out more at danielmcdermott.net.

ANSLEY MOON was born in India and has since lived on three continents. Her work has been published or is forthcoming in *Southern Women's Review, Glass: A Poetry Journal, Mascara Literary Review, PANK, J Journal* and various anthologies. Her book of poetry, *How to Bury the Dead,* will be released next year from Black Coffee Press. She currently lives in Brooklyn, New York.

CHRISTINA MURPHY lives and writes in a 100 year-old Arts and Crafts style house along the Ohio River. She continues to be amazed at how the Arts and Crafts movement—like painter Piet Mondrian—found such artistic integrity (and solace) in straight lines and simple (yet complex) forms. Her writing appears or is forthcoming in a number of journals including, most recently, *ABJECTIVE, A cappella Zoo, Splash of Red, LITnIMAGE, Blue Fifth Review, POOL: A Journal of Poetry, Blue Fifth Review,* and *Counterexample Poetics.* Her work has received an Editor's Choice Award and Special Mention for a Pushcart Prize.

JENNY ORTIZ is a 23 year old writer living and teaching in New York. When she was a little girl, Jenny wanted to be a gun-slinging drifter, much like a Clint Eastwood character. She ended up (happily) graduating from Adelphi University with an MFA in Creative Writing and is currently working at St. John's University and LaGuardia Community College. When she is not teaching or writing, Jenny can be found hanging out in IHOP with her friends, discussing music, video games, or *Avatar: Last Airbender.* When at home, she enjoys reading Haruki Murakami or listening to podcasts from the *New Yorker.* Follow her on Twitter: twitter.com/jnylynn.

JONATHAN PLOMBON is a writer based out of St. Cloud, MN. His essays and articles have appeared in publications such as *Paracinema Magazine* and *Video Game Trader*. A self-proclaimed semi-professional professional wrestling journalist, he has upcoming pieces on the sport that examine topics such as the struggles of openly gay pro wrestlers and filmmaker Fred Olen Ray's adventures in the squared circle. This is his second published piece of short fiction. His first, "May Date with Mariah Carey," was featured in *The Upper Mississippi Harvest*.

JONATHAN H. ROBERTS is a prolific writer of unpublished fiction, though a smattering of his stories have appeared in various journals, magazines, and anthologies. He currently lives outside of Indianapolis, Indiana, with his beautiful wife Andrea.

STEPHEN SCHWEGLER is the author of *Perhaps.*, a collection of incredibly insane short fiction. His work has been published by *Jersey Devil Press*, *Blink | Ink*, and *Short, Fast, and Deadly*. He was born on Long Island, but spent most of his life growing up in the wasteland more commonly known as New Jersey. He lives there with his wife and two cats who think they run the place. They do. He has an unhealthy affinity for movies, games and all things toast. Seriously, he has like four toasters.

DANGER_SLATER is highly-volatile and could explode at any moment! To be safe, don't use your Danger_Slater around open flame. Don't expose your Danger_Slater to direct sunlight. Do not look your Danger_Slater in the eye or you might turn to stone. Danger lives in New Jersey. The only devil he's ever seen lives in his bathroom mirror. It needs to cut its hair.

yt sumner likes words and people that write them. People that listen to them. People that read them. Eavesdroppers. Stutterers. Silvertongues. She was born in the UK, raised all over Australia and settled happily in Melbourne. Her short stories have appeared in various literary journals, anthologies and magazines and she's currently coaxing a motley group of them into a collection.

MIKE SWEENEY lives in Central New Jersey where he writes constantly but never quite enough.

RYAN WERNER is a Midwesterner. He has a body built for sin and an appetite for passion.

LOUIS WITTIG is a writer and editor who lives in North Jersey. His fiction has appeared in *Storyglossia*, *Prick of the Spindle*, *Dark Sky Magazine* and *Wag's Revue*. His nonfiction has appeared in *Alligator Juniper* and the *Concho River Review*.

www.ingramcontent.com/pod-product-compliance
Lightning Source LLC
Chambersburg PA
CBHW070916130626
46555CB00001B/164